For
John Harris
Mark Hebden
Max Hennessy
My Pa

Cetera Desunt

1

Chief Inspector Evariste Clovis Désiré Pel was not a happy man.

He was seldom happy, but this time he felt no one could blame him. During a recent raid on an HLM, *habitation à loyer modéré,* France's equivalent of council flats, where two amateur Arab bomb-makers were holed up, his handsome assistant Daniel Darcy had had his good looks rearranged by a rifle butt, leaving not many teeth but a very nasty taste in his mouth. Bardolle, the policeman built like a cart-horse, had had one of his massive shoulders dislocated, and Pel – beyond badly twisting an ankle, which he was convinced was broken – had also ruptured, he was sure, at least half a dozen of his suspected stomach ulcers. The only one to have come out of the whole business virtually unscathed was Misset who, having been knocked unconscious and spent most of the time slumped in a corner, had had his head X-rayed and been sent home with a clean bill of health. Pel was convinced the hospital had made a serious mistake; he was sure Misset had been suffering from brain damage almost all his life, if indeed he had a brain at all.

However, he had to admit, no one had been killed and there were now two new occupants at 72 rue Auxonne, by which name the local prison was lovingly known.

Pel looked down the list of men on duty that morning for a likely candidate on whom he could unload some of his dissatisfaction. Ticking someone off would make him feel better. Misset was the obvious choice, but there was little pleasure in having a go at him; everyone took it out on Misset if they could. Darcy, he decided, would have to be left for another day. Apart from losing his dazzling Disney smile, it was rumoured he had also lost his beautiful girlfriend and as a result his sense of humour too. Thank God for Nosjean, still looking like the young Napoleon on the Bridge at Lodi, intense and always in love, but a good cop – Pel couldn't find fault with the way he behaved, not that morning anyway. There was always the aristocrat of his team, known at the Hôtel de Police simply as de Troq', but Pel's bad temper, he knew, slid off the *vicomte* like water off a duck's back.

It would have to be one of his more junior officers. Annie Saxe, the only female member of the team, was a possibility. She had made a startling entry just before Christmas with her red hair and green eyes, and had been nicknamed the Lion of Belfort, not only because she actually came from Belfort, a once brave town near the Swiss border, but also because of the dynamic way in which she defended herself. She was a one-woman demolition squad when roused and, remembering what happened when Misset had tried to get frisky with her, Pel allowed himself almost half a smile. She didn't deserve a dressing-down either.

Debray was away on another course in computers, which left only the angel-faced Aimedieu, innocent-looking Brochard, or Didier Darras, his protégé. Having been the little boy next door in Pel's bachelor days, he'd finally grown up and had become a policeman, quite a good one at that. Pel sighed. He had nothing against any of them except that they were much younger than he was, and even Pel couldn't bring himself to have a go at them for that.

But of course! The two new boys, Pujol and Régal. They were still wet behind the ears in his opinion, but being terrified of their boss they tried hard to keep out of Pel's way. They were also terrified of Darcy, it seemed. Pel had caught them both whimpering behind the Sergeants' Room door and had threatened them with a fate worse than death if they didn't show a bit of loyalty. At last Pel relaxed, realising he'd already torn a strip off somebody that morning.

Although his ankle was agony Pel decided to try a bit of exercise, and taking the blue packet out of his drawer, where he had hidden it, he extricated a small white cigarette. If smoking was to be his only pleasure for the moment, then he would at least stop feeling guilty. With the pain he was having to endure he couldn't possibly give up smoking now. He lit the cigarette and luxuriously inhaled the smoke down to his socks, coughed violently and began to feel decidedly better. Even so, picking up the pieces of his bruised team was not going to be easy.

Not only that, the Chief was having a go at him to do a bit of sucking up to a rich American who had recently arrived in the area. The English and Dutch tourists were bad enough, but now he was being asked to tolerate Americans! The race who had invented the hamburger, Coca Cola and *Dallas*. For the love of God, whatever next? The Chief, however, had pointed out that this particular American had arrived in Pel's beloved Burgundy with a lot of money and was spending a great deal of it, much to the benefit of the local trades-people. In addition, he was thinking of asking planning permission to build a factory outside the city which would create almost a hundred jobs. The *maire*, on receiving this news, had become totally besotted by the American, and because unemployment was always a major problem, he was insisting that everyone, including the police department, was pleasant to him. And that meant Pel. Hence the Chief's request that he make a courtesy visit to Margay, *l'Américain*, their very own J.R.

But for the moment, he would have to wait. Pel had

other problems. For instance, his wife had left him. Not permanently, thank God, but for long enough to pay a visit to the fashion houses in Paris to organise the buying from next winter's collections. It had always been a cause for concern with Pel, that as soon as summer was on the verge of taking hold of the countryside, Madame was organising the next winter's woollies for her highly successful and very expensive boutique, next door to her equally successful and expensive hair salon, Nanette's.

With Madame away life was exactly as Pel had suspected it would be, dreadful. His former housekeeper, Madame Routy, who had been taken on and tamed by his wife, was now, in her absence, back to her old ways and terrorising Pel with the television turned up from loud to unbelievable and cooking inedible casseroles. Pel had taken great pleasure the evening before, as he often had in his bachelor days, in waiting until the last moment, then disappearing at a rapid hobble to dine in town, leaving Madame Routy to polish off her own burnt offerings. The war was on again!

Apart from all that, however, things were relatively quiet, with only the few hundred cases of breaking and entering, offences against public morals, non-payment of taxes, sale of alcoholic drinks to minors, drunken driving, bar room brawls, which were to be expected. And of course, the supermarket at Talant had been broken into again. But no one worried too much about that any more; it had break-ins like a dog had fleas.

There was only one other thing that was bothering Pel. It was a letter. A letter that had been badly delayed by the recent postal strike in France, arriving three weeks after it had been posted in Hong Kong. The writer was his old friend Professor Frédéric Henri, an archaeologist, who was scratching about in the hope of uncovering a bit more of China before it all changed hands at the end of the century. In fact, the Professor was not really that close a friend, although Pel had met him on a number of occasions in France, and while the Professor knew everything about Pel, as if he'd taken the trouble to research the subject carefully, Pel knew very little about the Professor, except that he liked him, an eccentric French academic married to a pretty English woman, who got on famously with his own wife. It always helped. They'd spent a number of happy hours putting the world to rights after a typically exhausting meal in the shade of the courtyard of one of Madame's numerous relations. For an academic, the Professor was quite a pleasant surprise to Pel. For a start he wasn't in the least bit boring, and Pel had finally admitted him to his bigots' society, of which he was founder, president and only member, after he'd completely condemned the world's politicians as utter idiots. Pel agreed entirely. After that they had got on like a house on fire.

The letter had Pel baffled, however. It had obviously been written hurriedly and consisted of very few words. 'Beware of Cats coming to France. I'll explain later. In the mean time, the Shrew should know of the missing Links. Got to do some more digging, but research going well. See you soon.' It was signed 'Fred'.

Pel couldn't make head nor tail of it, and he hadn't a clue who the Shrew might be. They'd just have to wait, he decided, until the Professor turned up to explain himself.

Pel settled down to a quiet day sorting the backlog of paperwork. But he was in for a surprise: the day was not going to be quiet at all. Within half an hour all hell had broken loose at the Hôtel de Police.

11

2

The Chief was the first to blast through Pel's door. He had
been a champion boxer as a young man and was heavily
built and still strong. He threw back the door as if he were
trying to tear it off its hinges.

'That's it,' he bellowed. 'The kite's gone up, and we're
in for it.'

'Please take a seat.' Pel was already feeling nervous,
but with the Chief towering over him he was feeling
claustrophobic too. 'What's happened?'

'Margay, the American – his house has been robbed.'

'When?'

'We don't know exactly. He got back from a trip to the
coast, and discovered a great deal of the contents of his
manor missing. Get over there, Pel, and see what you can
do. The usual teams from Fingerprints and Photography
were called in by the local gendarmerie early this morning. I've only just been informed. And take de Troq',' he
added. 'Perhaps he can smooth any ruffled feathers.'

It was true that Charles Victor de Troquereau de Turenne
was a baron, though he claimed to be impoverished, and it
was true that with his aristocratic manners and complete
self-confidence he was ideal for smoothing ruffled feathers, but when Pel called for him he was informed that de
Troq' was already out. Darcy looked as if he'd just stepped

12

from ten rounds with Cassius Clay, so it would have to be Nosjean. He was young, but an intelligent and excellent cop. Although he still blushed from time to time, much to Pel's delight, he knew how to behave.

The courtesy call had turned into duty and Pel was heavily resenting the interruption of his quiet morning.

'So, we're finally going to meet our famous Monsieur Margay.' Nosjean was obviously more impressed than Pel with the idea. He was driving at his usual mad lick and scaring the living daylights out of his only passenger, Chief Inspector Pel. 'Everyone's talking about him.'

'I'm not,' Pel replied, his knuckles going white on the dashboard as Nosjean swung fiercely round a tight corner. Having taken an instant dislike to the American, Pel was determined not to budge in his opinion. To change the conversation, therefore, he asked about Nosjean's fiancée, Mijo Lehmann. The reply was full of the usual concern Nosjean showed for his girlfriends. He fell in love easily, mostly with girls who looked like Charlotte Rampling or Catherine Deneuve, but Mijo, an antique's expert, whom he'd met during a series of château burglaries, seemed to have stuck, and they'd finally announced their engagement. Although Nosjean still felt he was too young to die he couldn't imagine life without Mijo and had finally succumbed to her requests, and those of his three adoring sisters, accepting that marriage was inevitable. He went on talking, as Pel had calculated, until Margay Manor finally came into sight.

The American's house was well out of the city to the south, the last three, kilometres winding through the beautiful vineyards of Burgundy. Vineyards that produced the famous Nuits-Saint-Georges, Beaune, Mâcon and of course Beaujolais. They stretched from the north to the south of Burgundy in a narrow strip, down the side of the auto-route, producing, as they always have, 'the best wines in Christendom'. Pel was proud of his Burgundy, and in the first few glorious days of July the sunshine threw a golden light across the acres of wine-producing fields, promising an excellent vintage for their remarkable wines. To Pel they were the only wines worth drinking and, glancing with half-closed, terrified eyes at his beloved Burgundian countryside, he almost sighed with pleasure. There was nowhere like it in the world, and even though at that moment it was hurtling past the window at five hundred kilometres an hour, it was still a wonderful sight. He hoped that all these damned foreigners buying up his precious homeland were not fool enough to try and tell the viticulturists how to produce wine – that really would be the end.

Before long they saw the manor on the next rise, an impressive house surrounded by a well established parkland with full mature trees. Until recently it had been rather tumbledown and the gardens overgrown. It had become the haunt of young couples in the spring, who availed themselves of the romantic setting to do romantic things to each other. Since Margay had signed the final Act of Purchase and taken possession, there had been a constant stream of lorries up and down the road, providing the materials for the local artisans to do their best and convert the manor back to its former glory, adding central heating for the winter, air-conditioning for the summer, and an enormous swimming pool with moving summerhouse, so that it could be either inside or outside depending on the weather. It was true everyone was talking of the rich American, particularly when he'd paid all the workmen in cash the same day they finished, plus giving every man a bonus for finishing on time. Pel decided he was a very flashy American.

Nosjean stopped the car, wheels crunching on the newly laid gravel, outside a huge double front door, obviously hand-carved in oak and almost a monument in itself. Before Nosjean had finished ringing the bell to one side the doors opened a crack and a small woman poked her head out at them. For a moment she blinked at their identification cards, then as if she had suddenly registered something important, she threw the door wide open and asked them to enter.

'I'm the wife of the Guardian, Monsieur Barrau,' she announced, wiping her hands on her flowered overall. 'It was my husband, you know, that discovered the robbery. He telephoned Monsieur Margay, and poor Monsieur had to come rushing back from the seaside. Down there on business, I shouldn't wonder, although it might have been for a bit of a holiday, one never knows, does one?'

There was a brief pause in her diatribe, long enough for Pel to ask if Monsieur Margay was in fact at the house at the moment.

'Oh yes,' she replied, 'he's here. They've all come back now, that's why I'm here. I've come in to do the cooking. They just love my French cooking.'

It seemed as if all hope was lost of stopping the constant flow: she was a small woman but suffering from a large dose of verbal diarrhoea. But she did stop, very abruptly, and turned on her heel to disappear behind what they assumed was the kitchen door. Turning themselves, both Pel and Nosjean saw the American. It had to be the American because he was just removing a large leather cowboy hat.

Margay was a big man, and like his house, handsome and imposing. Pel disliked him immediately. His hair was grey and perfectly groomed, as was the neat beard that covered most of his face. He invited them into a large drawing-room and as they settled into the comfortable furniture Pel noticed with horror that the man was wearing cowboy boots with high heels. He wondered where he kept his holster.

'First question, monsieur,' Pel started.

'Call me C.J.'

Pel wouldn't have dreamt of it. 'First question,' he persevered. 'Do you have a list of the missing items?'

'Sure, I already gave a copy to your fingerprint boys

earlier this morning, but I can let you have one too if you like.'

'I'd much appreciate it.'

'What's got us all puzzled,' Margay went on, 'is the alarm system, installed at great expense and the best on the market. It was working perfectly this morning when we tested it, so how did the critters get in and rob me, and get out without anyone hearing the siren? It's enough to blow your ear-drums inside out. I'll give you a demonstration.' He leapt to his feet far fuller of enthusiasm than Pel, whose ankle was hurting badly and who would have preferred to remain seated. However, a demonstration was on the agenda and Pel obediently followed the American out into the hall again. Nosjean passed a knowing hand over the head of one of a pair of magnificent leopard statues standing to attention on either side of the large fireplace, then followed his boss to participate in the alarm show.

'See,' Margay was saying, 'it's a very sophisticated system, all electronic beams and things. The moment someone enters a room, this little brainbox detects body heat and mass and off it goes.' He prodded a small button and Pel thought the world was coming to an end. Nosjean clasped his hands over his ears. The wail was agony. Margay mercifully switched it off.

'Quite impressive, don't you think?'

'Very.' Pel's ears were still ringing, and his ankle was hurting even more now. He glanced at Nosjean, hoping for a little sympathy, but he was staring up at two enormous paintings that dominated the entrance hall.

They all went back into the drawing-room and during the discussion that followed an immense limousine came to a halt outside the windows. It looked large enough to hold a game of football in.

'Only a hire car,' Margay explained, noticing Pel's raised eyebrows, 'but I do like moving around in comfort. I do a lot of travelling and I earn a lot of money, so I pay for what I want.'

The door to the room opened and two young men came in, both chewing gum but with plastic unwavering smiles glued to their faces. They were immaculately dressed in expensive lightweight suits, immediately making Pel feel like the man who had come to mend the lavatory.

'Let me introduce you to the guys. This is Bobby Patterson, my accountant, and G-G-Goldberg, my lawyer. Shake hands, guys.'

Both men stepped forward to present themselves, but a quick glance at Nosjean confirmed what Pel was thinking: they looked distinctly like a couple of well-paid heavies, the sort they would have expected to see standing beside their old friend Tagliatti, ex-gangster, before he finally met his maker. Or perhaps behind his replacement, Carmen Vlaxi, not quite as big in the crime hit parade, but rapidly rising to fame. The only thing the set-up lacked was a couple of beautiful girls. Behind Tagliatti and Vlaxi there had always been a beautiful girl and one could hardly have called Madame Barrau, the Guardian's wife, a dolly bird, with her damp apron and brown peasant's face creased into a permanent frown.

Having gone through the formalities and made their notes, Pel and Nosjean left. Outside they had to skirt round the limousine to Nosjean's little Peugeot. Pel wondered how it was that a good, hard-working, honest policeman had to drive around in a small and very often battered car, thinking himself lucky if he got enough time off to make a pass at his long-suffering girlfriend, and finally settling down in a small house with a pocket handkerchief garden, all of which was mortgaged to the hilt, leaving him in fear of bankruptcy every time the electricity bill arrived, while the crooks of the world swept about the countryside in mile-long Mercedes, and lived in luxury surrounded by bodyguards and beautiful girls.

All of this, he knew, could hardly apply to Margay. They

had no reason to believe he was dishonest even though the two young men looked like heavies. Perhaps American accountants and lawyers always looked like that. All the same, he decided he'd like to know more about their Monsieur Margay.

It was well past midday when they arrived back in the city so they stopped to eat rapidly at the Bar Transvaal just across the road from the Hôtel de Police. With his mouth full of *sandwich jambon*, Nosjean was leaning against the counter and telling Pel what he thought of Margay Manor. Pel had heard enough and seen enough of Margay and his manor for one day and was trying hard to concentrate on juggling a piece of pâté on to a crust of baguette. As he failed for the third time, wishing he too had ordered a simple ham sandwich, he realised what Nosjean was saying.

'What do you mean, fake?' he said.

'I mean exactly that. What was left in Margay's house, and admittedly there wasn't a great deal apart from empty spaces, but what was left was as fake as a plastic diamond.'

'Go on.' Pel had given up trying to spread the temperamental pâté and was eating it in small lumps with the torn-up bread to follow. He was suddenly less interested in what he was eating than in what Nosjean had to say. His involvement in a number of art frauds and thefts had given him a good knowledge of the subject, and he was well worth listening to.

'For instance, in the drawing-room, usually one puts one's best painting so that guests can see and admire it too. It makes your reception room attractive and furnished and you see it whenever you're relaxing. There were admittedly a number of blank spaces, but on the wall opposite the fireplace was an immense painting, too large to put in the back of a car or small van, if you were thinking of stealing it, so I presume that's why it was left. But it was a fake, a copy, not even a particularly good one. Same thing applies', he added, 'to the two monstrous pictures hanging in the entrance hall. Both fakes.'

3

When they got back to the Hôtel de Police there seemed to be a heated argument going on in the Sergeants' Room. There were a number of raised voices, each trying to out-shout the others. The subject under debate was Darcy. Pel stopped briefly to listen.

'He's worse than the old man!'

'That's not easy, and he's not even as old as the old man.'

Pel knew immediately who 'the old man' was, and was none too pleased to find that another member of his team could be worse than him. He took great pride on being the most over-worked and cantankerous in the department.

'He may have no teeth,' the raised voice continued, 'but –' The conversation was cut dead as Pel did his impression of the Chief, flinging back the door with a great deal of violence, so that it crashed against the filing cabinet behind. Pel was not as large as the Chief, but he knew how to make his presence felt. Framed in the doorway, his small black eyes glittering from behind his spectacles, he brought about an abrupt and complete silence.

'He may not have many teeth left,' he said coldly, 'but he's your senior officer, and a damn sight better cop than you lot. Now get on with your work. If you haven't enough come and see me immediately. I'll soon find you some.'

As Pel left the stunned occupants of the Sergeants'

Room to shuffle guiltily back to their business, Nosjean commented quietly, 'Well played, patron.'

Pel was, however, troubled by what he had heard. It was true Darcy had lost a lot more than half his teeth, and while Pel had tried to ignore the fact, this morning's complaint was not the first. It had brought the problem back to his attention and he made a mental note to see Darcy during one of their quieter moments. Perhaps one day before he retired.

'Well, what's this Margay like? Was there much damage at the house? What's missing?' The *maire* had been on the phone again and the Chief, normally a calm man, was feeling harassed. He was prepared to take it out on Pel. He knew from past experience that Pel was tough enough for the treatment.

'Margay', Pel replied unmoved, lighting a Gauloise and pushing the packet forward for any other sinner who cared to indulge, 'is an overgrown cowboy. He has high-heeled boots and owns a very silly hat. I think he wants to be France's answer to J.R.'

The Chief sighed, and sat down heavily in the spare chair. 'I gather you didn't like him?'

'Not particularly. In answer to your second question, there appeared to be no damage whatsoever, but no doubt Fingerprints will give us a few answers and make things a little clearer later in the day. And finally, there seems to be a great deal missing, according to this list Margay gave me.' Pel pushed the neatly typewritten list across the desk for the Chief to see. 'But', he added smiling, 'Nosjean has a feeling that it's not quite what it seems.'

'Inform me.'

'On the list you'll notice a number of impressive names,' Nosjean explained. 'A Toulouse-Lautrec pastel sketch, a small Degas painting of dancers, a couple of gold candlesticks, various porcelain miniatures, Wedgwood coffee

21

cups, Lalique glass and even a Fabergé egg. But from what we saw in the house there's not a thing left that's genuine. What's left is the large stuff, the sort of size that would be difficult to move and more difficult to sell. The furniture is all reproduction, quite expensive, even so, but nothing like the real antiques they're pretending to be. The two paintings in the hall are vast, and bad copies. The two leopard statues on either side of the fireplace are, too. I'm sure I've seen them on sale in one of those discount halls like La Foire Fouille. In a decent shop in Paris they'd cost five or six thousand francs a piece. At La Foire Fouille the mass-produced replicas cost no more than five or six hundred. They're only cheap pottery. You can tell when you touch them, and if you tap them with your fingernails it's obvious, they just don't make the same noise as porcelain or bone china.'

The Chief had had the wind knocked out of his sails. Their guest of honour had turned out to be a disappointment. 'I'd rather been expecting something a bit more exciting than a load of junk, considering what everyone says about this Margay. He's supposed to be extremely wealthy. I've had the *maire* on to me again this morning, saying we must clear up the affair quickly to restore Margay's confidence in the area. As you know, he's wanting to open a factory just outside the city which would create a lot of jobs for the locals. Our politicians and the Conseil Général, the Town Council, are very anxious to keep Margay and his money here.'

'Well, I'm not sure he's all he's cracked up to be,' Pel said. 'I'd like to know more about him. Like where he originally comes from, and how he made so much money. And who his friends are.'

'Pel, don't stir up trouble, just because the man dresses like a cowboy.' The Chief knew what Pel was capable of. 'After all, he is American.'

'That's no excuse. But don't worry, for the time being I won't ruffle any political feathers.' He did however make a note to get quietly in touch with Cousin Roger, an accountant in the city, who had on more than one occasion supplied him with very useful snippets of information.

Nosjean had been listening without saying anything, but now he came back to life. 'I've been wondering', he said, 'if it isn't an insurance fiddle.'

'Explain.'

'Well, we know little about Margay except that everyone's talking about him. He arrives in the area and buys a run-down manor house. The locals don't have the money to restore it and it's been on the market quite some time, so he gets it at a low price. I've checked with the former owners and they tell me they were obliged to reduce the asking price dramatically just to get rid of what they considered to be a near-ruin. He takes it over, renovates it to its former glory and installs himself and his belongings. He pays for everything in cash and makes quite a reputation for himself. As we know, it works – he's become the talk of the town. However, he's robbed of his so-called treasures. Nobody doubts that they are treasures – after all, he's a rich man, the colour of his money has already been seen. The insurance claim goes in for a vast amount, and if they pay up, hey presto, he's paid for the house, the restoration and more. All he has to do then is sell the house, saying he's disenchanted with the area, at an enormous profit, and he moves on the next one.'

'And the factory he proposes building?' The Chief wasn't to be put off so easily.

'It is only a proposal at the moment. It could just be a move to give the man credibility. Renovating houses can be a very profitable business,' Nosjean concluded, 'but with a hefty insurance claim for almost worthless contents as well, he'd be into big money. No wonder he's rich.'

'Don't let's jump to conclusions.'

'But it's certainly worth looking into.' Pel insisted that

it was a possibility. 'Check in other areas in case he's done it before, then find out what you can from the insurance companies. In fact, get Lage to do it. He's slow but he's thorough. It'll keep him occupied while he's waiting for his retirement. And while we're at it, get Misset to keep a watch on Margay Manor. Surely he can sit in his car and look in the right direction without making a cock-up of it. He'll complain, but ignore him.'

'Most of us do,' Nosjean admitted, grinning.

'And', Pel finished, 'let's find out if his plans for this factory are genuine, see how far they've gone.'

As the Chief left, he made one last request for discretion. 'I don't want things stirred up unnecessarily. You may be right, but until we can prove it, walk as if you're treading on eggshells. If the man's legitimate I don't want this department to take the blame for frightening him off and losing those jobs. This bit of France, like the rest of the world, needs them. And Pel,' he added, 'do something about Darcy, he's becoming intolerable.'

Darcy would have to wait. Pel had a great respect for him and he hoped that, if Darcy were left in his office to cool down, his face and his pride might recover. But Pel, this time, was wrong.

Nosjean had left Pel's office to put Lagé and Misset into gear, and to find out if Prélat of Fingerprints had come up with anything interesting on the Margay case, but he rapidly returned to give Pel some bad news.

'Darcy's gone too far this time, patron! He's just clouted Misset. Unfortunately, Misset lost his balance and his head made contact with a desk corner. He's been taken off to be stitched up. It looked quite nasty.'

It was true that Pel felt like congratulating Darcy instead of reprimanding him – there probably wasn't a man, or woman, in the department who hadn't wanted to thump Misset at some time or another – but it was also true that Darcy couldn't go around clouting fellow policemen just because he was in a bad mood. Even if it was Misset.

'Tell one of the youngsters to do the surveillance at Margay's place – Didier Darras, for instance, he's a bright lad. I expect Misset will need at least the rest of the year to convalesce. And tell Darcy I want to see him. And tell Fingerprints to hurry up.' The day was turning out to be even worse than Pel had first suspected. There was only one thing for it: he lit another cigarette.

Darcy and his still-bruised face appeared before Pel almost immediately.

'You wanted to see me, patron?'

Pel pushed his spectacles up on to his forehead, and put down the papers in his hand.

'Why did you clout Misset?'

'I didn't clout him, I gave him a shove, silly fool tripped over his own feet again. He deserved it.'

'I don't doubt that he deserved it. I've felt like clouting him on more than one occasion, but I didn't, and you shouldn't either. I can't have my officers bashing each other up. Now calm down and sit down.' He pushed the half-empty packet of cigarettes across towards Darcy. 'Have a cigarette, it'll sooth your nerves.'

'I've given up.'

'Don't be so stupid!' Pel wasn't having that. 'Take a cigarette.'

'Is that an order?'

'It's an order!'

Pel took a deep breath and studied Darcy as he lit his cigarette. His once good looks together with his pride were badly battered. His beautiful girlfriend had left him, and his glittering Disney smile was a wreck. Darcy's profile would recover in time, and – Pel hoped – so would Darcy. But policemen didn't have time to brood over personal unhappiness. There was a job to be done and Darcy would have to get on with it, teeth or no teeth.

'Daniel, you are making yourself very unpopular. It's time to pull yourself together. You're a good cop. Until now you've been one of the best.' Pel didn't usually hand out compliments, but he felt Darcy was in need of one, and anyway what he'd said was the truth. 'But', he continued, 'you're bitter, and a bitter cop is a bad cop.'

'I know all that, but look at me.'

'I don't want to hear it, Daniel. If you need some time off to sort yourself out, you only have to ask. You've been hurt, and it could be easily arranged.'

'Time off?' Darcy almost snorted. 'To do what? Brood alone in my flat? Wander about with nothing to do but wonder who she's going to bed with now and waiting for nothing to happen? There's no point.'

'Darcy! Stop moaning. Misset moaning I accept, we all accept, well, until today. Me in a foul mood, you have to accept because I'm your superior officer, but you in this state I will not tolerate.'

Darcy opened his twisted mouth to speak but Pel cut him dead. 'Quit it, Darcy!'

'Or?'

'Or quit the police!'

Pel had been hard on his assistant, but he was damned if he was going to watch one of his best men destroy himself for a set of teeth and a girl. Teeth could be fixed and there were plenty more girls in the world. Darcy, Pel had always assumed, would be the one to take his place when the time came. Now he was beginning to wonder.

Darcy disappeared, still looking morose, leaving the door open for Prélat of Fingerprints to enter. Nosjean followed him in. Pel felt as if he were sitting in the middle of the Champs-Elysées with all the traffic that passed in front of his desk.

'Well,' he said, 'what have you got for me?'

'Not a lot, unfortunately. The fingerprints we found belong to the occupants of the house, plus the Guardian, Barrau, and his wife. The intruders, like most of them nowadays, were careful to wear gloves. The alarm system was the same. It hadn't even been tampered with and appears to work perfectly.'

'It must have been heard by somebody, even above the television and across a couple of vineyards. That thing is loud enough to wake the dead. The Barraus would have heard it in their cottage.'

'The alarm is 120 decibels. Certainly it should have been very effective,' Prélat admitted.

'Apparently the Barraus didn't hear anything,' Nosjean said. 'They don't watch a great deal of television, the usual rubbish, *Sacrée Soirée, Stars 90*, Patrick Sabatier, that sort of thing, but after ten o'clock they're usually in bed. Barrau is the Guardian of Margay Manor, but he's also the farmer on the Margay estate. He's a peasant and lives by the peasant code, up with the light, home with the dusk, and early to bed.'

'Well, do we have any indication as to when exactly the robbery was committed? After all, Margay had been away for a week on the coast.'

'None, unfortunately. Unlike a murder, where rigor mortis is, or is not, present, a robbery has no tell-tale signs to give us a clue. It could have happened any time during his absence.' Prélat knew he was being less than helpful to Pel, but he had no choice. 'And another thing, we can't find the point of entry. There were no broken windows, forced doors, anything of that kind. The only thing we believe we've established is where they got out. The kitchen door is always locked from the inside and the key kept in a small basket on the windowsill. It's not easily visible from the outside as there is wax fruit in the basket. However, the door was locked but there was no sign of the key. We found it eventually in the shrubbery on the other side of the drive. It's my belief that they went out by the kitchen door, knowing where to find the key once they were in the house, then carefully locked up so as not to rouse suspicion and tossed the key into the bushes.'

'So it must have been someone who knew the house well?'

'Or someone who had worked there,' Nosjean suggested. 'Let's face it, there have been dozens of workmen at the house over the last few months. It would only need a big mouth in a bar and everyone in the district would know where to find the key to the kitchen door.'

'Under the wax fruit. Not even the fruit is genuine,' Pel commented drily.

'Yes, but that was getting out, after the crime had been committed. Presumably what they stole went out the same way?'

Prélat agreed. 'But we still don't know how they got in, unless they had the front door key as well.'

'In which case they would have used it to go out again. Why bother opening the comparatively small kitchen door if the large front door was already open? You could drive a tank into the entrance hall with those double doors wide open.'

Pel considered for a moment. 'No dried mud, no footprints, no dropped packets of matches with phone numbers on them, no stubbed-out Russian cigarettes, nothing that one would expect James Bond to come across?'

'Nothing, not even the vaguest footprint. One would think they took off their shoes.'

'Wonderful! Such a help.'

As they were leaving, Pel suddenly remembered his academic friend in Hong Kong. He called Nosjean back and handed him the letter he'd received from Professor Fred.

'What do you make of that?' he asked.

'Not a lot,' Nosjean admitted, looking baffled. 'I haven't got a clue, and anyway, who the hell's the Shrew? That's a new one to me.'

Pel sighed. They were getting nowhere. 'That's what I wondered.'

The phone rang and Pel reached out to answer it as Nosjean replaced the letter on the desk and left. To Pel's surprise, when he put the receiver to his ear, it was his wife.

'What a pleasant surprise,' he said. 'Where are you?'

'I'm on my way home, Pel. I thought I'd ring you and find out how you are. I still think you should have taken a few days off to give your ankle time to heal properly.'

It did Pel's heart good to know there was someone in the world who cared about him, particularly a woman as attractive and successful as his own wife. His own wife! Even now it startled him to find that he was married to an intelligent and loving woman, and it startled him even more to discover that after all this time she still loved him. At first he thought she hadn't shied away because, with a certain amount of vanity, she had removed her Chanel glasses and perhaps hadn't seen him too well. But now he knew she had seen him for better and for worse, even first thing in the morning with his sparse hair standing on end, and that was definitely the worst, and she still cared about him. Wonders would never cease. He was a very lucky man.

'What time do you think you'll be home?' he asked, trying to put a bit of adoration into his voice, but succeeding in sounding dyspeptic. Fortunately Madame Pel knew her husband well and was not put off.

'In about an hour. I'll have your whisky waiting for you.' Her voice was music to his ears. 'That is, of course, if you think you'll be able to get away in reasonably good time.'

Pel decided that whatever happened, even the second storming of the Bastille, he was going to be home in reasonably good time. Loyalty to the police was one thing, but a good woman, especially a woman as good as his own wife, deserved a bit of loyalty too, and anyway he'd missed her. That apart, he was also longing to see the look on old

Routy's face when she discovered she couldn't terrorise him for another evening as she'd expected.

As he left the building a little later, he saw de Troq' in the corridor. Being a baron he had had an education with a certain finesse that most policemen lacked. Pel was by now fairly convinced that the mysterious Shrew in the Professor's letter wasn't a criminal they knew. Records had turned nothing up. Perhaps he was a well-known character in literature and would be a clue to the rest of the message. He thought he should therefore try it on de Troq'.

But de Troq' just shook his head like Nosjean. 'The only Shrew I know of is in a play by Shakespeare.'

'How very interesting,' Pel replied. 'Thank you for nothing.'

De Troq' grinned and wished him a good evening, unperturbed by Pel's usual sarcasm.

4

It was delightful driving home knowing that his wife would be there to greet him instead of just the sour-faced house-keeper, Madame Routy. For the first time that day Pel felt as if all was almost right with the world, particularly in his beloved Burgundy. The golden light of early evening was changing to a rich orange, making paint splashes across the clear skies as the sun sank slowly towards the horizon. For once life wasn't letting him down, even though he was confronted by an infestation of cowboys. Well, he knew there was only one of Margay, but it was a start, one never knew where it might lead. It could be the beginning of a flood of millions, all wearing high-heeled boots and sporting silly hats, and then where would they be?

His whisky was waiting as promised as he entered the house, along with his wife. He immediately limped a great deal; sympathy, he felt, would make him happier. They sat together in their attractive *salon* sipping their drinks and quietly discussing what had been happening since Madame had left for Paris. Although it had only been the day before, to Pel it had seemed like an eternity. Madame Routy, he was pleased to note, was crashing, though only mildly crashing, about in the kitchen, and the television was blissfully silent.

'How's poor Darcy?' Pel's wife asked. She'd always had a soft spot for Darcy since it was he who had finally brought Pel and his wife together.

'Suffering.'

'Poor Darcy,' she repeated. 'Can't we do something for him?'

'He's doing it all for himself at the moment,' Pel replied and went on to explain how he'd clobbered Misset that afternoon.

'Oh dear. Isn't there anything he can do on his own for the time being? To give him time to recover? I know police work is teamwork, but perhaps he'd be better away from the others for a while.'

It was a good idea, but his wife was very right in saying that police work was teamwork: it would be virtually impossible to isolate Darcy.

Madame left to join their housekeeper in the kitchen to put the finishing touches to their evening meal, and Pel, throwing caution to the wind, served himself another whisky – a small one, he said to himself, but somehow his hand slipped and it ended up being a double. However, he could hardly pour it back into the bottle, most likely he would spill some and that would be wasteful, no good Burgundian liked waste, so, resigning himself to indigestion, he took his second glassful into the garden to enjoy the last of the warm evening sunlight.

As was often the case he found his young neighbour, Yves Pasquier, by the hole in the hedge with his dog that looked like a mop head. Once again Pel greeted the wrong end; it was always difficult to tell which way it was facing.

'Hello, Monsieur Pel. Had a hard day?'

The boy had extraordinary perception, Pel thought. 'A bit, but it's getting better.'

'How's the ankle?'

'Agony.'

'There's *Star Wars 2* on television tonight,' the boy went on enthusiastically. 'I'm allowed to stay up and watch it because it's Tuesday and we don't have school tomorrow.'

Pel had never quite understood why French schools closed every Wednesday. It must be the poor teachers, he imagined, always overworked and underpaid, and never enough holidays, he mused sarcastically. He would have enjoyed working the hours of teachers with all that time off. But, on the other hand, then he'd have no excuse for avoiding working in the garden, and he'd also have to suffer a classroom of rancid-smelling children almost every day. He got on well with small boys, one at a time, but a whole classroom! Perhaps police work had its advantages.

Yves was busy outlining the history of *Star Wars* 1 and 2. Pel wasn't very interested in outer space, the earth on which he lived was quite enough for him, but Yves had changed the subject slightly without Pel noticing.

'Yes,' he was saying, 'at Toulouse. They're going to send up a European weather satellite and the Communauté Européen have chosen Toulouse to be the centre of surveillance. Good, isn't it? Great for us to have the responsibility in France, and not give it to the Rosbifs in England or anyone. Mind you, they've got a Rosbif in charge all the same. Monsieur Incks, he's called. Funny name, ever heard of him?'

'No, never,' Pel said, still not sure what the boy was on about.

'Well, I'd better go in now, it's due to start soon and I've got to have a bath first. I don't really like baths, do you?'

Pel looked startled. It had never occurred to him to like or dislike the daily ablutions; they had simply become a habit which he went through more often than not on remote control.

'I hope you enjoy the film, Yves. Tell me about it the next time we meet.' Pel always treated youngsters with the utmost respect. They, he found, were not in the least bit stupid. It was when they grew up they often turned into prize idiots.

*

Madame Routy had surpassed herself for Madame's return. When she wasn't there her cooking was a singed nightmare, but the moment Madame came back, she showed talents in the kitchen Pel had never known she possessed in all those years she had kept house for him before he was married.

The Boeuf Bourguignon was excellent, the salad was fresh and the Camembert almost walked off the table on its own. Perfect! Pel was feeling very mellow. He and his wife retired to the comfort of their English-style armchairs with a small Armagnac each. Pel showed her his mysterious letter from Hong Kong, but though she studied it for quite some time, she had no suggestions as to its meaning.

'Ask Darcy,' she said finally. 'He's got a good brain for deciphering things and always finds the right place to dig for information.'

Pel's head had just touched his pillow and he was sighing contentedly when the phone beside him shattered his peace. Immediately Pel had a sinking feeling in the pit of his stomach. He knew it wasn't the whisky or the Armagnac, it was a feeling of impending doom.

'I'm sorry to disturb you, patron,' Darcy said, 'but I thought you'd like to know. We've got two murders on our hands.'

Pel knew it had been too good to last. Sadly he kissed his wife good-night and left for the city.

5

The first murder to have been reported was that of an old lady who lived in a ground-floor council flat on the outskirts of the city. By the time Darcy and Pel arrived, Nosjean was already there together with Fingerprints, Forensics and Doc Minet from the Path. lab.

'Inform me,' Pel said as Nosjean met them at the front door.

'The dead woman's name is Marty. It was a neighbour who found her. She'd been out visiting her own mother and had stayed to put her to bed. When she came in through the front door of the block of flats she noticed that this flat had its door open, which was unusual considering the time of night. The old couple went to bed early. She knew them quite well, and thought simply that they'd closed their front door badly, so she went to pull it to. It was then she heard the gurgling.'

'Gurgling?'

'The dead woman's husband is bedridden and paralysed from the waist down.'

'So there's a witness?' It seemed like an unexpected stroke of luck.

'Yes and no . . .' Nosjean hesitated. 'Not only is he paralysed, but he's also blind and hasn't spoken in seven years. The best he can manage is a gurgling noise, which is what Madame Odent, the neighbour, heard. It wasn't often he made any noise at all and she felt something must be wrong. She went to fetch her husband who was asleep in front of the television.'

'I don't suppose he'd heard a thing?'

'Not a thing, even though they live in the flat above. Anyway, they both came back, went into the flat and found the old lady on the floor.'

'I'd better have a look,' Pel said and entered the tiny flat which was now very crowded with all the experts necessary for a murder.

Photographs were being taken from every angle. Doc Minet was still bent over the body, Leguyader of Forensics was poking about on the floor of the dining-room beside the body, and Prélat with an associate from Finger-prints filled the rest of the space. In addition to all these people in the little dining-room was a large double bed where the dead woman's husband lay, alive but silent.

'Minet's been in touch with the hospital,' Nosjean explained quietly. 'They're coming to take the old boy away. Minet thinks that he may well be aware of what has happened although he couldn't have seen anything. He's totally unable to express himself and could be suffering from shock. If only he could tell us something.'

'Can he write?' Darcy asked on the off-chance that it might just be the answer to all their prayers.

'Let's get him out of here first,' Pel suggested. 'Nosjean, make a note to see him in hospital tomorrow. Find some-one from the family who may be able to understand his gurglings. And offer him your notepad and pencil, just in case.'

Doc Minet got up from behind the dining-room table and looked at Pel, then at the old man lying motionless on the bed. He shuffled round towards him, trying to keep out of everyone else's way. 'I'd like to talk to you,' he said to Pel, 'but let's go into the kitchen.'

They both took three steps to the right and found them-selves in a minuscule kitchen. It was no bigger than an

36

overgrown cupboard, and it too was vastly overcrowded with furniture and electrical appliances.

'I don't suppose we're out of earshot at all,' Minet whispered, 'but the old boy is in a bad enough state as it is. His wife died almost beside him. She was killed by a knife wound just behind the ear. She would have died almost immediately – the blade made contact with the base of her brain, making very little sound. I'll tell you more when I've made my examinations in the lab, but I think I can say fairly confidently that the murder weapon was a stiletto knife.'

'A stiletto? We don't get that sort of thing on our patch normally, do we? It's more a sicilian weapon, surely?'

'You may be right, but I'm pretty sure that's what killed her. She appears to have no other injuries.'

Leguyader joined them in the kitchen looking slightly puzzled. 'I can find no sign of a struggle. Nothing's been broken, nothing disarranged, apparently nothing stolen, although we can't be sure yet, but there are no open drawers or cupboards to indicate someone searching. All we have is a dead old lady with a hole in her neck. I may be able to tell you more later, but I doubt it.' There was a hint of glee in his voice. Leguyader and Pel had indulged happily in their own private war for many years and the man from Forensics took great pleasure in either having nothing to tell Pel at all, or boring him rigid for hours on end with his expertise in an effort to prove that, without him, Pel would never solve a single case. Pel was forced to tolerate him because he knew very well that Leguyader was good at his job.

A SAMU ambulance had appeared in front of the swing doors of the block of flats, from which came two men, dressed in their navy blue combinations and red kepis, bearing a stretcher.

'Come to fetch an old boy to hospital,' one of them said cheerfully; then, seeing the milling crowds behind the flat door, he stopped and stared. 'Mon Dieu, what's been going on here?'

'Inform him, Nosjean,' Pel said, and turned to leave. The thought of two more people, plus a stretcher, jammed into the already overcrowded rooms made him think it was time to see the second case.

Although it was well after midnight by the time they arrived to see the other murder, there was a good crowd gathered at the bottom of the flight of concrete steps leading up to the apartment. Pel, for the hundredth time in his career, wondered where they had all appeared from. They should all have been in bed, or at least watching the end of *Star Wars*.

Darcy and Pel pushed their way through the crowd and went up the steps to see de Troq' waiting in the doorway. Pel gestured at the staring faces below them.

'Are any of this lot witnesses?' he asked.

'No, just sightseers.'

'Then get rid of them. This is not a football match, it's the scene of a crime, and they should be in their own homes. If necessary, take everyone's name and address and tell them we'll be in touch.'

This murder was different. It was messy. Pel didn't like guns or blood, and he had a feeling he was going to be seeing a lot of the latter. The whole small apartment was upside down, with smashed crockery covering the tiled floor; in the room at the end of the hall he could see overturned chairs and a smashed coffee table. The corpse, however was in the bedroom to the left of the front door. It was that of another woman, not as old, but definitely as dead. She was half wrapped in bedclothes as if in her last moments of life she had clutched at the covers in an attempt to save herself. At her feet was a broken lamp, and there were large bloodstains at intervals along one wall, as if her murderer had bounced the dying woman along it trying to extract some information from her before she gasped her last breath. Her face was also covered in blood and badly bruised, her short dyed blonde hair was red and matted with the blood from her wounds, and in her hand she clutched a small saucepan, bent round the edges.

'She was trying to defend herself, I think.' Darcy spoke quietly as they all did when faced with the gory details of violent death.

Having seen the body they went back into the slender hall and on into the kitchen beyond. Sergeant Aimedieu was sitting at the table amongst the debris of the flat questioning a weeping woman in curlers. She was clutching a handkerchief and at regular intervals blew her nose loudly into it.

Aimedieu rose from his chair as he saw Pel, who waved to him to sit down and continue, while he stood to one side and listened.

'It was Madame Gimat who found the body, patron,' Aimedieu explained. 'The dead woman's name is Lucette Lafon.'

'Known as Lulu au Lit, Lulu in Bed,' interjected Madame Gimat. 'She had a bit of a reputation, you know.' Again she blew her nose ferociously then looked up to concentrate on Aimedieu.

'What time did you hear the disturbance, madame?' he continued.

'I don't know, I can't remember. I do know that we were tired. My husband works late sometimes and he'd come home in a bit of a mood, so we'd eaten and gone straight to bed. Then she started. Well, I thought it was the usual thing.'

'What would that be, madame?' Pel asked.

'Well, she's been married a couple of times, and sometimes one of her ex-husbands would turn up and they'd start shouting at each other. If it wasn't them it would be one of her other men friends the worse for drink. There was always a man turning up late and making a noise.

I shouldn't say it, I know I shouldn't, what with her being dead and all, but she wasn't an easy neighbour. More than once we've had words about the noise. But she just told me to mind my own bloody business and shut the door in my face. Well, it was my business,' she went on, looking from Aimedieu to Pel and back, hoping for understanding, 'if we can't get a decent night's sleep because of . . . because of her goings on.'

Aimedieu gently brought the woman back to this evening's events.

'Tonight I heard shouting. My husband was already snoring, but I woke him up to listen. It was louder than usual, and I was fed up. We lay there for a long time waiting for it to finish.'

'How long?'

'Half an hour, I suppose, then I'd finally had enough. My husband wouldn't do anything, he just put his head under his pillow, silly sod, and started snoring again. But I was wide awake and in the end I couldn't stand it any more. So I got out of bed and came round. The door was ajar and the lights were on, but suddenly there was no noise. I knocked on the door but got no reply. I was in such a state I just barged in. I was going to have it out with her once and for all. I came in here, past the bedroom door, you see, because the light was off in there, but it was on in here. Well, I called out but there was still no reply, then I realised I was standing in all this broken crockery, and the chairs were all over the place. It gave me quite a turn, I can tell you. I got out quickly and went to fetch my husband. When we came back we turned on all the lights, and, well, then we found her, over by her bed, all twisted up in the corner. And . . .' She brought her damp handkerchief up to cover her mouth in horror. 'She was still warm.'

Again she blew her nose noisily, as if trying to rid herself of the memory.

'You heard shouting almost until you arrived on the doorstep?'

'Oh yes, sir.'

'Then I think, madame, you were very lucky,' Pel commented. 'From what you say it is very possible that the murderer of Lulu Lafon was still in the flat when you came in the first time. He could have made his escape when you left to alert your husband.'

'Oh my God.' The woman wrung her hands, looking terrified.

'By the way, where is your husband now?'

'One of your policemen took him home. He couldn't stop throwing up.'

6

The meeting at the Hôtel de Police the following morning was a sober affair, not least because many of those present had had little sleep that night. Everyone was there, including the Chief. As usual their criminals were being most inconsiderate, not giving the police time to clear up one investigation before they started something else. The Margay robbery was still brand new and now they had two murders on their hands. There was going to be no time off for a while and Pel's team knew it.

'Firstly,' Pel started, 'the Margay case is at least under way. Lagé is making enquiries to find out about the insurance claim, and Didier Darras, you are to continue to watch the house. De Troq', I want you in charge of this one. It'll please the *maire* to know there's a baron on the job. Get a list of all those concerned with the renovations and go and see them. You never know, it may be a simple case of greed. Well paid for what they'd done at the house but unable to keep their sticky fingers off the valuables. Find out if there was an architect involved – he'll be able to supply you with the list of firms, and they'll tell you who the workmen were. If not, find out from the Guardian, Barrau. He should know just about all the firms, especially if they were local. In the mean time, go and see his wife, Madame Barrau, and find out exactly what was going on at the house while Margay was on holiday. Callers, deliveries, Jehovah's Witnesses, tramps, that sort of thing, I want to know exactly who's been in the house, even who's been up to the front door.'

De Troq' made his notes as Pel continued. 'You can have Brochard.' He glanced in his direction. 'Being a farmer's son you'll know how to handle the locals around the area. If you need more help, there's big Bardolle too, he still got his shoulder strapped up but he'll want to be useful.' From beneath his bandages Bardolle nodded his agreement. Pel looked sternly across his desk at him. 'But keep your foghorn voice under control. They've already got an alarm system.'

He paused to light a much-needed cigarette before moving on to the two murders.

'For the time being,' he said from behind a thick cloud of blue smoke, 'I'm waiting to hear from the various experts, but we'll want statements from all the neighbours, just in case they saw or heard anything that'll give us a lead. I don't expect anything, people seem to walk around with their ears and eyes shut, but we can always hope for a miracle. Nosjean, you'll need men to cover the ground, so take who you need. Be thorough, all those fools standing about gaping last night must have been vaguely awake to have come to watch, you never know.'

Nosjean finished writing and looked up. 'I've got to see Monsieur Marty, the old boy they carted off to hospital, too.'

'Leave that until this afternoon. I'd like to get going with what was seen and heard. It's my belief that the neighbour at the second murder may have disturbed the murderer when she went round to complain. She touched the body after coming back with her husband and found it was still warm. The Path. lab will confirm it, but she must have just died.

'Aimedieu, you're to work with Nosjean on that one as you took the original statement, and for the interviewing of the women you'd better have Annie Saxe along. Find out about their families and friends, any strange visitors during the last few days as well. They're a nosy lot in the council flats usually – you may just turn something up.'

As they all rose to leave, the Chief quietly asked Pel what he had in mind for Darcy. It had been noticeable that he had given him no instructions.

'I've something quite apart for Darcy. He's been bawling out the Sergeants' Room again this morning, so he's got a special assignment.'

Before Pel had time to see Darcy he was confronted by Judge Brisard, who appeared in the corridor, puffing with the effort of climbing the stairs, and followed him into his office. Out of the 555 *juges d'instruction* in France, Pel thought, why did he, Evariste Clovis Désiré Pel, Chief Inspector of the Police Judiciaire of the République of France, calmly going about his business in Burgundy, have to suffer Brisard the Busybody?

He was an overweight lawyer, with wide woman's hips. He had a strong line in family harmony and kept photographs of his wife and children permanently installed on his desk, but to Pel's certain knowledge he also had a woman in Beaune, a policeman's widow, to be precise. Brisard knew Pel knew and it didn't help their already strained relationship. Brisard, in turn, considered Pel touchy and quarrelsome; more than once he'd found him lacking in respect for his own position. However, they had to work together. Brisard had the right to interfere in Pel's enquiries, and even to make his own investigations if necessary, to bring the prosecution of a serious crime to trial. Pel resented any interference, particularly from a pear-shaped, pious man like Brisard, and although they managed to remain polite, sometimes they both found it difficult.

Pel was finding Brisard difficult that morning as he stood before him, clutching his files to his over-round stomach. Already the sun was streaming through the large windows of the Hôtel de Police, turning the offices into ovens, and Brisard was perspiring abundantly.

'Fastidiousness and rapidity,' he proclaimed to Pel, passing a plump hand over his damp forehead, 'that's what is needed. The murders of two innocent women in one night are not good for the city. This could cause a panic. You must conclude your investigations quickly.' He paused, breathing heavily, waiting for Pel's reaction.

It was slow. Pel had decided to take his time in answering, choosing his words carefully, knowing he was in danger of snapping unnecessary expletives which he had learnt by past experience would do no good but merely antagonise Brisard into a further pompous speech. Although Pel was indifferent about antagonising him, now was not the time or place. He thought, if I stay calm perhaps he'll go away and leave me alone.

'I quite agree,' he said finally. 'We must have this cleared up satisfactorily as soon as possible. My men are already out on the streets asking preliminary questions and gathering information. I think you can expect results in the not too distant future.'

Brisard was surprised and impressed. Even Pel was impressed. Particularly as all he'd said was that the enquiry was underway, but it had sounded very good.

'Perhaps, in view of the urgency,' Pel concluded, 'I should proceed with the calls I have to make.' He gave Brisard one of his dyspeptic smiles, replaced his spectacles on his nose and bent over the papers in front of him, reaching for the phone in the same movement.

'Indeed, indeed.' Brisard nodded approvingly and closed the door silently, almost reverently, as he left.

Pel smiled to himself. For the first time he'd succeeded in throwing Brisard the Busybody out of his office, and the best of it was that the pompous old fool hadn't even noticed.

Now for Darcy.

*

'Darcy! Stop sulking!' Pel threw the packet of cigarettes across the desk at him. 'I haven't given you any of the existing cases because I've got something more important for you. Or at least,' he added, 'I think it may be more important.'

He handed over the Professor's letter, which Darcy studied for a moment.

'Who's the Shrew?' he asked.

'That's exactly what you're going to find out. I've asked around but no one has any suggestions to make, except my wife. She was the one who thought you might have the brains to decode the message. In fact, if you need a starting point, it may well be worth going to see her. On the few occasions I met the Professor we did a great deal of talking, but rarely about ourselves. Our wives, however, I feel sure, will have discussed the families – you know what women are like.'

'I used to think so, but now –'

'So go and see Madame Pel,' he interrupted Darcy rapidly before he could feel sorry for himself. 'The Shrew isn't any criminal we know. I've tried records and found nothing. He could be a member of the Professor's family, or at least known by one of them. He has children, I think – they might be able to help, if you can find them.'

'I'll see what I can do,' Darcy replied. 'I presume you need results by yesterday.'

'Probably, but until we've found out what the message means we're still a bit in the dark. I can't tell you how urgent it is. So get on with it, but take care not to miss something that may be important.'

Pel didn't realise it, but he'd already missed something himself. De Troq' had already given him the answer.

Towards the end of the day Leguyader and Doc Minet came to see Pel with their reports on the two murders.

'This is a curious one,' Doc Minet said, laying his files

on the desk and drawing up a chair. 'I didn't spot it at first, but Leguyader did.'

He would, Pel thought – he was a veritable walking encyclopedia. He expected an hour-long speech from Leguyader on the intricacies of his job. But he was happily surprised when Leguyader finally finished fiddling with his notes and spoke.

'I can see you're very busy, Chief Inspector, so I'll come straight to the point.' It would be the first time, Pel thought. 'It's a very fine and very sharp point to be precise,' continued Leguyader in his slow careful manner. 'The point of a stiletto knife, to be exact.'

'We knew Madame Marty was murdered with a stiletto last night,' Pel said, sighing, wishing the man would get on with it.

'Indeed you did. I believe Doc Minet told you when you arrived at the scene of the crime. However, what you didn't know, and what we've just discovered, is that although the second woman, Lulu Lafon, looked as if she'd been clubbed to death with a blunt instrument, in fact the wounds to the head were superficial, enough to cause substantial bleeding, as you saw, and a bad case of *traumatisme cranien*, as her murderer bounced her head against the bedroom wall – you will remember the bloodstains?'

'Yes, so?' Pel's patience was already wearing thin.

'So, as I was saying, although the woman was severely injured, she was in fact killed by a knife wound just under her ear. A knife wound that penetrated her lower brain.'

Pel removed his spectacles and reached for his cigarettes, staring at Leguyader. 'Exactly the same as the Marty woman,' he said.

'Both women have the same punctures in their necks and penetration to the brain. Yes, exactly the same method of murder. Not only that,' he continued brightly, 'the depth and angle of the fatal wounds were identical, which may suggest to you the same murderer.'

47

'But Lulu Lafon put up a good fight from the look of her flat. How is it that a struggling woman could have an identical wound inflicted as an old lady who apparently didn't struggle at all?'

'Because, by the time the fatal wound was inflicted, the Lafon woman was unconscious on the bed. From the bloodstains on the sheets and mattress I deduced that she had first collapsed there. Hair soaked in blood makes a particular pattern, and as she had already suffered considerable loss of blood, and was by this time terrified, we concluded that she had fallen there unconscious. While lying motionless on the bed – and she would have been motionless, the bloodstains are not smeared to suggest further movement – the blade of a stiletto knife was introduced into her neck and punctured her brain, hence causing instant death. As her head was released, her body slipped with the bedclothes to the floor.'

'And the time of death, what about that?'

'Not long before she was found. Rigor mortis was not present, and from the position of the remaining blood in her body I would say the time of death was around midnight. She was, as you know, still warm when first discovered.'

'So it's highly likely that the neighbour did disturb the murderer when she went round the first time?' Pel's mind was piecing together what he was being told and building up a picture of what had happened the previous night.

'It's possible,' Doc Minet agreed.

'The lamp beside the bed has been tested,' Leguyader added. 'It wasn't working when the body was found, but it only had a broken bulb. It was fitted with a new bulb and found not only to be working, but switched on.'

'Broken in the struggle,' Pel said to no one in particular. 'Conveniently, it now seems, or Madame Gimat might just have gone into the bedroom and found herself face to face with the murderer. As it was, it was in darkness, and she had the sense to get out and fetch her husband, giving the murderer time to escape, and saving her own life.'

'By the way,' Doc Minet interrupted Pel's mental calculations, 'Lafon was killed only forty-five minutes after Madame Marty.'

'And by the same weapon.'

'So we're looking for one person,' Pel suggested, 'who murdered Madame Marty, and possibly with the information he or she had got from her, went to see Lulu, beating her up to find out more, or to collect something of value, and finally killing her so she couldn't talk.'

'It looks very likely,' they agreed.

'So what's the connection between the two women?' Pel asked himself.

'That I can't tell you,' Leguyader answered smugly. 'I only deal in facts.'

Pel felt like throwing his filing tray at him.

When Nosjean came back into the office that afternoon, Pel sent him down to see Forensics. Although he'd briefly explained the situation himself, he preferred him to hear it directly from the lab, if only to see if he came to the same conclusions.

Nearly the whole of Pel's department was out and about in the city making their enquiries. Only Lagé was still in the building, contacting all the insurance companies in the area. He'd started off with those in the city, but had had no luck in finding Margay's insurers. Now he had moved further afield, and was realising very quickly that he would have to attack the massive Paris directories. Didier Darras radioed in to ask if his surveillance of Margay Manor should continue into the evening and was disappointed to be told that until the house had closed its shutters for the night, he was to stay where he was. He only hoped that the American knew that all good French families shut their shutters as darkness arrived, late though that would be, it being summer.

Darcy had disappeared after making a number of phone calls, and Pel sincerely hoped that he had a lead. The fact that he'd left his office seemed to indicate that he was getting somewhere.

Unfortunately he was wrong. Darcy had drawn a blank and, finally giving up, had gone to the city library in the hope that the librarian might be of some help. He had successfully made an appointment to see Madame Pel, but not until the following day. She had been out of her office at the time and one of her assistants had made the appointment.

Pel was surprised to find that, soon after Darcy had left, Misset had turned up looking very sorry for himself. It was almost as if he'd been watching the main entrance waiting for his aggressor to leave. Finding there was no one in the Sergeants' Room but Lagé, who was permanently attached to the phone anyway, and could therefore offer no sympathy to the suffering Misset, he mistakenly decided to try Pel.

'What do you want?' Pel snapped when he saw who had been feebly knocking at his door.

'I'm reporting back for duty.' That surprised Pel even more. Misset looking for work – it was incredible. He suspected, however, that he had had another row with his wife, and that she'd set the dog or the children, or both, on him.

'That's very noble of you,' he said, 'but I really feel, as everyone feels, you'd be better off at home, convalescing.'

The fact was that Misset's wife's mother had come to stay, as she often did, and a usually unpleasant home atmosphere had turned into a living hell. Misset preferred to duck out of sight and pretend that, even though he was dramatically wounded while investigating a very important case, the department needed him to clear it up. His wife and her mother weren't taken in for a minute. They knew Misset as well as Pel did.

'I heard about the two murders, patron,' he begged. 'Surely there's something I could do?'

'Yes, you can get out of my office, you're making the place look untidy. Go and be quiet in the Sergeants' Room – you could man the incoming calls. Lagé keeps being interrupted and he's trying to do something useful.'

7

Coming down the hill from his house the following morning, to join the main road near Talant, Pel was thinking about the three main cases they were working on. He failed to see an emerging lorry and missed it by the skin of his teeth. He left on the road behind him five kilos of rubber and an irate lorry driver mouthing his full repertoire of swear words at the tail end of Pel's car. Pel knew he wasn't a good driver, often being preoccupied with things far more important, and now he'd had the fact confirmed yet again. He found driving nerve-racking, particularly when his always active mind was wrestling with the problems of Burgundy's crime rate.

The man on the desk looked up as Pel entered the Hôtel de Police, and wished him a good morning. Pel ignored him, in fact he hadn't even seen him. The desk sergeant was used to Pel first thing in the morning and simply shrugged and continued with his paperwork.

There had been a sudden summer downpour that morning, falling from the sky like stair rods. It had caught Pel unawares and he was distinctly damp round the collar. Considering the possibilities of having flu in July, a good start to the season, Pel was preoccupied with drying himself with his handkerchief when the Chief called for him. Gathering about him a pyramid of files and enough cigarettes to last most people a year, Pel headed for the Chief's office.

'Wet this morning, isn't it, Pel?' The Chief was already pouring two cups of strong coffee from his personal coffee machine. Too late, Pel thought, I shall just have to drink it now.

'Thought we could have a quiet chat about Margay before the day gets into gear and rushes you off at a thousand kilometres an hour.'

Pel didn't in the least want to discuss Margay first thing in the morning. Cowboys and coffee mixed together were sure to give him indigestion for the rest of the day. He sat down, however, knowing that he was obliged to do so.

Taking a sip at his coffee and eyeing Pel from behind his cup, the Chief wondered where to start. He knew Pel well; he was an excellent detective, with a fast-growing reputation that was good for the department, as well as for the Chief himself, but he could be a difficult little bugger and sometimes it was worth trying to be tactful. If Pel decided to be obstinate it would be unpleasant for everyone concerned, not least of all for the Chief who was on the receiving end of pressure from the *maire* and their local politician. And now the American Embassy.

He carefully put down his cup and decided to take the plunge. 'I had a call from someone at the American Embassy late last night,' he said. 'He seemed concerned about the robbery at Margay Manor.'

'Really?' Pel registered disinterest.

'Apparently Margay is well thought of in some high circles and they are concerned for the recovery of his art treasures.'

'If they *are* art treasures, and not just a load of junk.'

'Well, yes, that remains to be seen, but I have the impression that Monsieur Margay is considered an important citizen of the United States of America and we should consider him as such here in France.'

'To me,' Pel replied haughtily, 'he's a man whose house has been broken into. He is therefore entitled to the same expertise and time to find his intruders and to recover his belongings as any man who has been robbed. Whether', he added silkily, 'he's a cowboy or a peasant.'

'Pel, I'm asking you, no, begging you, to make an effort,' the Chief said in desperation.

'Chief, de Troq' is the man handling the case. I think that if anyone in my team knows how to behave, it's de Troq'. He's a good intelligent policeman and I have complete confidence in him.' Pel finished his coffee and collected his unopened files. 'Will that be all?'

The Chief sighed and let the little bugger leave.

Pel had, however, taken notice of what had been said. Although it annoyed him, he had, all the same, decided to have a word with de Troq'.

'I think then you'd better go and see Margay personally,' he said as de Troq' presented himself in Pel's office. 'Ask him outright for the name of his architect as you had no luck with your enquiries yesterday – you might even find he's willing to tell us who his insurers are. Lagé is still at it, but going through the Paris directories could take him the rest of the year and into his retirement. I'd like this little episode cleared up quickly so that we can concentrate on more important issues.'

De Troq' nodded and turned to leave. 'One more thing,' Pel added. 'Find out from the Chief the name of the type who phoned from the American Embassy. You could let him know that we're making progress. Don't tell him what sort of progress because for the moment it's leading us nowhere, but it'll keep him happy for a bit. Oh, and de Troq', be careful to present yourself properly to all those concerned. Your full title, with all the frills, that should impress them for twenty-four hours at least. It'll give us time to get on with some work.'

Before de Troq' left with Brochard to see Margay, he called briefly back into Pel's office.

'Bob Sittingwell, patron, the chap who claims to be

from the American Embassy,' he told him. 'They've never heard of him. I phoned the Consulate's office and they couldn't help me. He could of course be someone very unimportant working there, like a junior secretary to a junior secretary . . .'

'Or the tea boy,' Pel suggested.

'They have a large staff in Paris,' de Troq' continued, 'and the juniors change regularly. He certainly had a strong American accent. The Chief had some difficulty in understanding him, although he spoke good French.'

'Or', Pel said, 'he is simply another American in France who Margay got to stir things up a bit. Well, at least we don't seem to have the Ambassador on our backs. Leave it for the moment and get on with the rest. We don't have time to worry about obscene phone calls to the Chief. He's big enough to cope. When are you going to the manor?'

'Consider me already gone,' de Troq' replied.

'Don't forget your title when you introduce yourself. I want Margay impressed and silenced for half an hour.'

Pel was right. After de Troq' had presented himself at the front door of the manor as the Baron Henri-Victor de Troquereau de Turenne, Detective Inspector of the Police Judiciaire of the République of France, adding for good measure a neat aristocratic click of the heels as he finished his announcement, Margay was indeed silenced. But only briefly. Recovering himself, he extended his hand to both de Troq' and Brochard, who was humbly waiting his turn behind the baron.

They were shown into the vast drawing-room with its immense oil painting and leopard statues on either side of a huge fireplace. De Troq' was inclined to agree with Nosjean: none of it was genuine. And when, after they had refused a beer, the coffee came on an ornate oriental tray, carried in by the simpering Madame Barrau, he also noticed that, although the spoons were very pretty and

55

almost too delicate for Brochard to cope with, they were definitely not real gold. De Troq' could tell just by the feel of them.

However, the interview was a success. Margay was obviously as impressed as he was supposed to have been by a real French baron's presence, and quite happily told de Troq' the names of both his architect and his insurance company, adding with a laugh that they might be in for a surprise.

'If you'd be kind enough to keep the amount of the insurance claim under your hat, I sure would be grateful. It might just give old mother Barrau and her gossiping friends a fright. She's bad enough already, but she's useful and a darn good cook. Because I'm loaded she's certain what was stolen is worth a fortune, but the whole goddam lot was fake.' He roared with laughter at his own private joke.

He roared with laughter again when Bob Sittingwell, from the American Embassy, was mentioned. He seemed to do a lot of roaring with laughter.

'Good old Bob!' he shouted. 'He's just a guy who called in briefly while he was over from the States. I told him about the break-in while we were talking, but I never asked him to stick his oar in. Nice of him, though, I must confess. Don't suppose it'll do any good – that Chief Inspector of yours, what's his name, Pel, he seems a bit of a cold fish, unimpressed by anything.' Pel, as usual, de Troq' thought, had made his presence felt.

'But you, my dear Baron,' Margay went on, 'I think you and I understand each other.' De Troq' wasn't so sure, but he smiled affably to give Margay the idea he was on his side.

'Both firms, the architects and the insurers, are in Paris,' he told Pel when he got back to the office. Neither would give any details over the phone.

Pel was already collecting up notepads and pencils, and the inevitable spare packets of cigarettes in case of an emergency. 'Then we'd better get up there and see them,' he said. 'If we set off now, we can be knocking at their doors when they open at two o'clock. We'll have something to eat on the way.'

Pel hated Paris and the Parisians, but there was a job to be done so they left almost immediately in de Troq's large roadster with its leather belt over the bonnet and headlamps as large as lighthouses. Although de Troq' claimed to be an impoverished aristocrat, Pel felt that poverty was comparative, and to him de Troq' always looked and behaved like someone with cellars full of money. Sometimes it was a great advantage having him on his team. Sometimes it was a pain in the backside and made Pel feel like the poor relation.

The insurance company was cagey, and still hesitated over giving details of the claim Margay had made. Eventually, when Pel had pulled his weight and explained that the Baron de Troquereau had come directly from the Manor, with the agreement of Monsieur Margay, they finally relented and supplied what was needed. As the detectives had been warned about the amount, it was no surprise to find that, although it was a substantial sum, it was certainly not enough to cover original paintings or a single genuine Fabergé egg.

'It's enough to replace the stolen items,' a snooty-looking young man pointed out. 'The originals, I am told, are in the States, under lock and key. He had the copies made to make him feel more at home at his French residence. A very honest and charming gentleman, I found,' he concluded, returning the papers to his files. The two detectives looked at each other. Pel was of the opinion, unfair though it may have been, that Margay had never even seen the originals, let alone possessed them. De Troq', as it happened, was thinking exactly the same thing. But the claim was correct and they certainly couldn't accuse Margay of anything fraudulent.

The architects were delightfully helpful. A pretty young secretary found the information quickly after confirming with her boss that she was allowed to do so. While photocopies were being made of the list of firms who worked at the manor, a man with untidy hair and an equally untidy face ran out of his office to join them.

'Sorry I couldn't see you and give you the information myself, but I'm in an important meeting.' He glanced back at his door where cigar smoke was beginning to seep out round the edges and through the keyhole. It smelt like quite a party. 'I just thought I should make sure you've got all you want,' he gasped. 'My secretary is an efficient little thing, she should be able to answer your questions quite satisfactorily.'

They agreed.

'No problem with the work that was done, I hope?'

'Not at all,' Pel reassured him, 'but there's been a break-in, nothing too serious, but naturally we must follow it up. The obvious place to start was with the men who had been in and out of the house over the last couple of months.'

'Of course,' the architect nodded. 'Usually we employ one firm of building contractors in Dijon, who come in and take over lock stock and barrel with their team of monkeys, as we call them – that's what they look like when they're climbing all over the outside of a house. But this time Monsieur Margay wanted to give the work to small local firms and we simply acted as supervisors in his absence. We had of course drawn up detailed plans for the renovations and we liaised regularly with the workmen. Surprisingly it was very straightforward.'

'Did the other firm, the one you usually use, show any animosity?'

'No. I think they were a bit surprised when they heard, but I pointed out that the new owner was an American and perhaps rather eccentric, and they seemed to accept it with no bother. They know they'll get the next contract for any French owners and they aren't lacking in work, so I don't think there was any problem.' He turned and glanced back again at his office door where raised voices could now be heard. 'If you'll excuse me,' he finished, 'I'd better get back. If there's anything else, ask my secretary, or if necessary you can always contact me by phone.' With that he ran back to his meeting and slammed the door.

8

While Pel had been in Paris with de Troq', Darcy had been to see Madame Pel.

He was greeted courteously at Nanette's, the famous hairdresser's belonging to Pel's wife, and was immediately shown up the flight of stairs to where Madame had her office. It had been in this office, Darcy remembered, that he had persuaded the widow Geneviève Faivre-Perret, as she was then, not to judge Pel too harshly and to give him another chance. Shortly afterwards their marriage had been arranged.

'Dear Darcy.' Madame rose from her desk removing her elegant glasses to receive him. 'How are you?' What a silly question, she thought, as she noticed that he'd affected a twisted smile to hide his broken teeth.

'Hurting slightly,' he replied, 'but I must say it's a pleasure to see you again, madame.'

'Let's sit down. Perhaps you'd like something to drink to help ease the pain?'

Although Darcy didn't usually drink spirits during the day, this time he made an exception and accepted a small pastis well covered with water.

Pel had been right in thinking that his wife would know about the Professor's family. She was very fond of both him and his neat English wife, Elizabeth; they had become good friends.

'Although the Professor is a Frenchman, they spent

many years in England and both children were educated there. First at what they call a prep school, then at public school, which is actually a private school.'

Darcy look confused, but Madame carried on. 'They have only two children. Their son, also called Frédéric, qualified as a doctor and finally joined Médecins Sans Frontiers, you know, the organisation who sends medical teams all over the world to help with disasters, earthquakes, wars, that sort of thing. Where he is at the moment I have no idea, so that's not much help, I'm afraid. But Cathérine, their daughter, might be a better bet. She married an English lord and lived in a castle somewhere between the north of England and Scotland until a few years ago.'

'What happened a few years ago?'

'His lordship, her husband, became a Member of Parliament. It so displeased Cathérine that she up and left him. I don't suppose for a moment that it was as simple as that, but she packed her bags and her two small sons into the car and left. She's never been back since.'

Darcy listened attentively, sipping his pastis, as Madame went on. 'I know her mother was very worried about it all. She thought that her turbulent daughter had finally settled down and accepted being a wife and mother. After she left they had no news at all. But Cathérine had inherited her father's spirit of adventure and was determined to get along on her own. Her father tried hard to hide his pleasure when she left her husband, but it was fairly obvious, even to me, he was pleased she'd escaped what he considered a life of drudgery and nappies. It wouldn't surprise me if he'd known all along where she was, perhaps giving her financial help to establish herself elsewhere. You know, the Professor is just like my Pel on the subject of politicians – they dislike and distrust every one of them.'

'Where did the daughter turn up eventually?' Darcy found the high-spirited Cathérine intriguing, hoping very much that he might have the opportunity of meeting her.

'Oh, but she's here in France! She came home to her father's country.'

Darcy decided this was the break he was looking for. 'Do you know exactly where she is, madame? I think it would be very helpful to speak to her.' Also possibly a pleasure. At long last he seemed to be making progress. Not for long, however.

Madame Pel shook her head. 'Oh dear,' she said, 'if only I could remember. I'm sure I was told, but you know, one doesn't pay attention to small details like that when you're in the middle of a friendly conversation about families.'

'Was anything said about the region that could give us a clue? Like the wine, the birds even, seagulls or buzzards? The climate, famous buildings, for instance?' he added hopefully. Darcy had met the Professor and his wife only once but still had a clear picture in his mind of Elizabeth. A true English rose, blonde and blue-eyed, even in her fifties she had been a beautiful woman. Perhaps her daughter looked like her? On the other hand the Professor was black-eyed, black-haired, and had a face that looked as if it had been struck by lightning . . . But Madame Pel was still shaking her head delicately. They were getting nowhere again.

'Wait a minute!' Madame suddenly exclaimed, after thinking hard. 'There is something that might help, but it's not much.'

'Never mind, tell me anyway.'

'The Professor's wife loves art and she told me about an exhibition she went to see in a town near Cathérine's home. Now what on earth was the name of the artist?' She paused, deep in thought again. 'Yes, I remember, it was Toulouse-Lautrec,' she said triumphantly, 'but it wasn't in Toulouse, or in the village of Lautrec.'

Darcy was delighted. 'No, madame,' he said smiling,

'it's in Albi, about two hours' drive from Toulouse and an hour from Lautrec.'

'Good grief, how do you know that?'

'If you remember,' he explained, 'my mother is from Toulouse and I was taken with my grandparents to see the house where the artist lived, and where there is a permanent exhibition of his works. I was only a teenager and I think they hoped to interest me in a bit of culture, but I'd just discovered girls so it was a useless attempt. However, I do remember where it was.'

Both Madame Pel and Darcy were pleased with themselves.

'I don't suppose', Darcy added hopefully, 'that the name "the Shrew" means anything to you?'

It hadn't when Pel had shown her the letter, and unfortunately it still didn't. It had been too much to ask for, but at least Darcy had something to work on. It wasn't a lot, but it was better than nothing.

As Darcy was leaving Nanette's in the city, Brochard was arriving at the Barraus' cottage, just across the vineyard from Margay Manor. On his way past he'd noticed Didier Darras installed on the hillside opposite dressed in bohemian clothes posing as a local artist with an easel in front of him and brandishing a number of paintbrushes. Somewhere under his paint-splashed smock was hidden a pair of binoculars which he lifted to his eyes every time a vehicle arrived at the manor. To Darras' disgust, it wasn't often and he was beginning to believe that an artist's life was not a happy one. It had stopped raining; however, the downpour that morning had sent him scuttling for cover in his ancient Deux-Chevaux car parked behind a clump of trees. Now the visibility was better, but he was still feeling soggy and not a little disillusioned with what he had first thought would be an easy job out on surveillance.

Brochard knocked at the door of the Barrau dwelling. There was no bell, although his arrival had been announced loudly by a large and vicious-looking mongrel chained to his kennel in the yard. Leaping at the visiting policeman and almost throttling himself on the end of his chain, his front legs off the ground, he curled back his lips to reveal a dangerous set of snappers. While the chain held, Brochard wasn't worried. All the same, he was quite eager to get inside.

It was obvious that some attempt had been made to renovate the house. Margay, he presumed, the tatty house being part of his estate, but although the tiles on the roof looked clean and neatly laid, and the guttering was brand new, the scrap iron and rusting machinery left about the place did nothing to enhance its surroundings. Just beyond the front door he noticed the inevitable enclosure where several ducks and a number of scruffy chickens scratched about looking for grain. An attempt had been made to modernise, but there was no feeling of affluence here as there had been at the manor.

Madame Barrau opened the door at last, wiping bloody hands on a grubby cotton cloth.

Brochard introduced himself in case she'd forgotten who he was, but she seemed to remember.

'Just gutting a couple of chickens,' she announced. 'You'd better come in out of the sun. Mind, I hope you haven't got a weak stomach – there are *tripes* all over the place!'

Laughingly she stood back to let him in, and in her merriment, Brochard noticed that at one time she must have been quite attractive before the life of a farmer's wife had lined her face and the weather beaten her skin to look like tough leather.

Brochard's young innocent face creased into a smile: the kitchen was a home from home. 'I was brought up on a farm myself,' he assured her. 'A dead chicken or two won't bother me. In fact, if you find me a sharp knife, I'll give you a hand.' He removed his jacket, hanging it over the back of one of the simple wooden chairs, then, rolling up his sleeves, he attacked the second limp carcass on the scrubbed table top.

'We've got the family again this weekend,' Madame Barrau told him, plunging her hand almost up to the elbow inside her poultry's rear end. 'Ever since we've been taken over by our rich American they seem to think we're rolling in money too. But you know, we still have to work for a living,' she went on, extracting a large bundle of intestines. 'Oh yes, there's the vineyards to cope with, fifteen hectares of grain, and now of course there's the house to clean and tidy, and the garden to tend. Most particular they are, those Americans. Want everything like you see it on *Dallas* and *Santa Barbara*.'

Brochard had never had the time to follow either of the famous *feuilletons*, but he could well imagine what she meant. Madame looked up for a moment at the young policeman, smiled her approval as he expertly removed the innards from his chicken, then went back to her own.

'I can see you're a farmer's lad,' she said. 'I can tell you know. Not like that baron chappie the other day. He was a bit posh for me, all full of airs and graces, he was.' It was true, thought Brochard. De Troq' had laid it on with a shovel, but it had been deliberate and aimed at Margay, not at his housekeeper.

'He's all right,' he replied, 'when you know him. He's just an ordinary bloke like me under all that title. He's my senior officer, so he gets to drink coffee at Margay Manor. Me, I'd rather talk to my own kind. That's why I'm here,' he explained. 'You're a very alert and intelligent woman. I think you can help me.'

Madame fell for the compliment immediately, and collecting up the mess from the table she wrapped it in newspaper and deposited it in the bucket under the sink, in order to give him her full attention. Brochard washed his hands while Madame cleaned the table, waiting for her to finish before sitting opposite her and getting down to business over a cup of coffee that tasted like iron filings and was so strong he could have stood his spoon upright in it.

'What I would like to know,' he said, 'is who visited the Margay house while he was away. I noticed that you can see the front of his house from here, so you'd see anyone arriving or leaving.'

'Nobody went to the manor, nobody at all. I like to keep an eye on the place, so whenever I can I have a quick look, but the place was shut up fast all the time he was away.'

'Did you go down there?'

'No. I never go into empty houses. They give me the creeps. I clean up and take away the laundry as they are leaving and go in to make the beds when they come back. No, not me, I didn't go in there.'

She frowned and was silent for a moment, leaving Brochard to sip at the disgusting coffee. She seemed to be trying to drag something from the back of her memory. 'My husband did though,' she said at last.

'When was that?'

'Friday night. The family was here again for a free meal. My husband's two brothers came over with their wives, rowdy lot they are and they eat enough to feed an army. The menfolk were still at the table talking, or rather shouting at each other, when us women had finished the washing up. I don't like men's discussions when they've been drinking, so I switched on the *télé* and we settled down to watch. It's not often I watch the television, usually too tired, but well, with my sisters-in-law there, I could hardly go to bed and leave them downstairs. Anyway, after a bit, my husband started to shout for the *digestives*, but we'd got nothing left, they'd finished the last of the brandy the week before. Not even a drop of *eau-de-vie* in the house. So he gets up from the table and says, not to worry, I'll borrow a bit from the Margay cellars, and off he goes. I didn't

66

stop him because I don't suppose Monsieur would notice if one of his hundreds of bottles was missing – anyway, he can afford it.' She winked at Brochard who, replying with one of his charming smiles, let it be understood that he understood. 'Every job's got to have a little perk,' she explained, 'and he came back a little later with a couple of bottles, all pleased with himself.'

'Was the alarm working when he went to the house?'

'I wouldn't know about that, you'd have to ask him.'

A dirty old tractor came to a noisy halt in front of the house, narrowly missing the end of Brochard's car as it jerked to a stop.

'Speak of the devil, here he is.' Madame Barrau got up from the table and flung open the kitchen window. 'How many times have I told you not to bring that thing round here? It blocks the view across the valley.' To Brochard she added, 'And then I can't keep tabs on the Americans.' She giggled to imply she was joking, but Brochard knew she was deadly serious. A peasant's life was a hard one with no holidays and Brochard knew only too well that, like his mother, Madame Barrau – along with looking after the house, the cooking, the vegetable garden and the poultry – must often have found herself working in the fields when extra hands were needed. Spying on the Americans was probably one of the few small pleasures she was allowed, a little bit of *Santa Barbara* at first hand.

Barrau, however, ignored his wife and came directly into the kitchen to shake hands. His boots were thick with mud and made sticky footprints across the tiled floor. He didn't seem to notice and Madame said nothing, simply putting the evil black coffee back on the stove to stew some more.

Barrau removed his beret and scratched his balding brown head. The deeply engraved lines on his face told the story of his life, under fire constantly from the baking sunshine or the biting winter winds.

'Got to keep the vineyards clean,' he announced.

'Grape-picking is in a couple of months and doing it in a tangle of weeds and brambles only makes it more difficult. The *vendange* is hard enough as it is, a real kidney-killer, does your back in good and proper, and I suffer all year round. Thought I'd have a couple of hours' break this afternoon, give the old bones a rest.' He laid his dusty beret on the table and took the bowl of coffee his wife handed him. 'What are you here for then, lad? Policeman I suppose, by the look of that fancy radio in your car.' Not much escaped Barrau's little ferret eyes.

Brochard explained why he was there, and also repeated what Madame Barrau had said.

'She shouldn't have told you that,' the farmer replied, scowling at her. 'It wasn't stealing. I'll tell Margay about the bottles, and I'll pay him if I have to.'

'I'm not worried about the bottles,' Brochard reassured him, 'that's not why I'm here. What I'd really like to know about is the alarm.'

'What about the alarm?'

'Was it working when you arrived and did you reset it when you left?'

'I'll tell you something, lad – if I was a burglar, I'd have run for my life when I heard that thing. It hurts your ear-drums. When you unlock the door there's a ten-second delay, so you can switch the thing off, but I was a bit slow, heavy-footed that night, and I managed to trip over the door mat as I went in. The alarm went off and scared the living daylights out of me. It didn't ring for long, mind, because with that noise I was pretty quick to switch the bloody thing off. Even my brothers heard it from up here. They'd stepped outside for a smoke.'

'I should think so too, disgusting habit.' Madame Barrau obviously wouldn't have appreciated Pel's company for long.

'My wife won't have them in the house, cigarettes that is, not my brothers.' Barrau laughed mildly at his own wit.

'I'm none too keen on *them* either,' she told him indignantly. 'They eat too much, they drink too much, and they stay too late.'

'The alarm?' Brochard suggested before the two of them rolled up their sleeves and prepared for a full-scale battle.

'I switched it off and went down to the cellar, collected the two bottles, came back up, switched it on again and left.'

'You're sure you switched it on again?'

'I'm sure. I went to put the bottles with my boots on the doorstep where I'd left them. They were my working boots, a bit mucky you see, I didn't want to leave footprints in their posh hall . . .'

'You don't bother about your boots here,' Madame snorted. She had noticed after all.

'Here's not there,' her husband replied without looking at her. 'So I put the bottles down, I remember, because with them in my hands I couldn't manage the keys and all. I went back into the hall and switched on the alarm, it did its little bleeping noise to show it was ready, then I went through the door, locked it, put my boots on, collected my bottles and came home. The whole thing must have taken between ten and fifteen minutes between my leaving and getting back – my brothers had only smoked a couple of cigarettes apiece.'

'And you've seen no one else at the house at all during Margay's absence?'

'Nope.' Both the Barraus were sure.

Brochard had made his notes carefully so that he could repeat exactly what had been said to Pel. 'And Margay reported the break-in on Tuesday morning when he got back from the coast, 'he said, thinking aloud. 'That means the robbery will have occurred between late Friday night, after you locked up again, and early Tuesday morning when Margay returned.'

'No, it was before that.' Brochard looked up at Madame

69

Barrau. 'Oh yes,' she confirmed, 'my husband calls into the house – well, opens the door – every day of the week, on his way home from work, just to check. He hadn't been in on that Friday because his brothers came over. That's another thing about your brothers,' she added accusingly to her husband, 'they arrive too early.' She turned her attention back to Brochard. 'But he went into the house that night, as we've said. Saturday and Sunday he didn't bother – well, we've got to have our weekend too, haven't we? But Monday, as usual, he went in on his way back for lunch and that's when he found the stuff missing. There's a little picture of a girl with no clothes on that used to hang in the hall, by the drawing-room door – you liked that one, didn't you?'

Barrau shrugged and hid behind his coffee.

'He noticed that was gone immediately. So he started looking a bit further. Came home in a right panic.'

'But you didn't report it?'

'Yes, I did,' Barrau said from behind his bowl. 'I reported it to Margay just like I'd been told to do if there was any trouble. He always left me a phone number. Fussy about that, he was. Even when he was in America. If anything happens, he said to me, ring me at once, and he told me to use the phone at the manor so I wouldn't have to pay for the call.'

'When you told him, what did he say?'

'Nothing really, just that he'd come back. He arrived that evening in a helicopter. We watched it land on the big lawn in front of the house.'

'But he didn't report the burglary then either?'

'If you say so. With him back in residence it was no longer my problem.'

When Darcy called in late that evening Misset was still manning the phone. He was feeling decidedly sorry for himself. With everyone busy he was getting very little

70

sympathy, but it was better than being at home under fire from the machine-gun tongues of his wife and his mother-in-law. Trying to be Burgundy's answer to Maigret wasn't all it was cracked up to be and when he heard Darcy's voice on the line he almost slammed the phone down again. However, thinking it would be more interesting to know what he was up to, he went on listening and took down the message for Pel.

Finishing writing, he read it through. 'You were right about your wife. Going south.' (Here he'd forgotten the name of the town, so he left it out.) 'Will be in touch. Darcy.'

Intriguing, Misset thought. Was Darcy following Madame Pel around? He knew Darcy was working alone on something no one knew anything about because he'd asked. Could the Chief Inspector be having problems with his wife? Darcy had found out something about her. For a moment Misset felt sorry for Pel – he'd been a long time getting Madame to the altar and now it looked as if it was all for nothing. Misset knew what marital problems were all about. He suffered from them constantly. He imagined what the patron would be like when he found out his wife was being unfaithful. No one would be safe, least of all Misset. He decided that being a man of the world he'd have a word with Madame Pel himself. He'd try and straighten things out discreetly. Gallantly he tore up the message into tiny pieces and let the confetti fall into the waste-paper basket.

9

The Chief joined Pel and his team for their daily conference early next morning. Nosjean was already there armed with his files, which were beginning to look depressingly thick. De Troq' was still working his way through the lists of workmen at Margay Manor, but had come into Pel's office to listen in for any ideas that might be forthcoming. Brochard and Aimedieu were also present to make their reports. Darcy was very noticeable by his absence. Pel had no idea what had become of him and although he'd tried his home number several times had got no reply.

Always anxious about the Margay case, the Chief suggested that Brochard should make his report first.

'The alarm was working while Margay was away. Barrau had been to the house on Friday night and it was heard across the vineyard at his own home. When he left he was careful to reset it. I'm confident that this is the case. When the alarm was tested on Tuesday morning it was working perfectly. No one had been to the house in Margay's absence except Barrau, who went every day to cast an eye, that is every day except Saturday and Sunday, his days off. However, what is interesting, the robbery was discovered by Barrau on Monday morning.'

'Monday?' Pel pushed his spectacles up on to his forehead and stared at Brochard. 'It was only reported to us on Tuesday.'

'Yes, patron. Barrau discovered a number of items missing on Monday morning. But as he'd been specifically instructed by Margay to tell him if anything untoward happened, this is exactly what he did. Margay arrived that evening by helicopter.'

'By helicopter? He must have considered it an emergency, not just untoward,' Pel commented. 'Do you have the phone number Barrau used?'

'I do and I've checked it. It's a big hotel in Montauban, not on the coast as he'd told the Barraus. I also followed up the helicopter and discovered it too had been hired in Montauban. He left the airfield at the army barracks just outside the city at 1745 that afternoon. It flew directly to Margay's front door, or at least the lawn in front of the house, then returned to Montauban. The controller looked it up in the log-books at the airfield. He couldn't give me the time of arrival here at Margay Manor, but the Barraus said it was early evening, the sun was still hot.'

'So why didn't he report the break-in that evening?'

'That I haven't found out yet. I thought perhaps it would be better if de Troq' questioned Margay.'

'He must have been checking whether something was still there before he called the police,' Pel said. 'Either that or hiding something he didn't want us to find.'

'Pel!'

'Chief, it's a possibility. I know that Burgundy and our big boys want Margay whiter than white and loaded down with dollars, but we have to explore the facts as we find them.'

'Just as long as you don't overdo it.'

'Have you any idea why he kept it to himself until the following morning?'

The Chief didn't want to admit it, but he had a feeling Pel might just turn out to be right about Margay. Not reporting the break-in immediately was indeed odd. He changed the subject. 'Have we any leads as to who may have done the job?'

De Troq' looked up from his lengthy lists supplied by the architects in Paris. 'I've been through all the names,' he said. 'There are a couple of likelies: Dupont, Jacques, he was in trouble for shop-lifting in his youth, but clean ever since. Larroque, Jean-Claude, arrested three years ago, suspected of breaking and entering a number of expensive flats in the city, but nothing was ever proved. I've even got the name of one of the men who did the supermarket at Talant some time ago, but he seems to be going straight now. There are a couple of others that may be of interest, like Giorgio Bargiacchi. He's a bit of an unknown quantity and is proving difficult to trace. But I'm checking and rechecking everyone, their whereabouts and their activities. It's taking time, but either I'll rule them out or eventually we'll turn up a probable.'

'Let's hope it's the latter,' Pel said, realising the Chief had successfully avoided his question. 'By the way, does young Darras have anything to report? He's been out watching Margay's house quite some time now. What's he got to say for himself?'

'Two things,' de Troq' replied, consulting his files again. 'Firstly, he says Margay has changed out of his fancy dress outfit. Apparently, he arrived at the house in his limousine dressed like an ordinary businessman. He went into the house then after a couple of hours came out again and was driven away in the same limousine that had brought him. The driver was one of the two men permanently in residence at the manor, either Patterson or Goldberg. He thought it strange however, because, although the car came back again later, he couldn't see Margay in it, but he did see Margay in full cowboy regalia strolling round the garden late that evening, just before they pulled all the shutters to and locked up for the night.'

'Perhaps he's just an ordinary businessman after all?' the Chief suggested brightly.

'The other thing,' de Troq' went on, 'which will be of

great interest to everyone, is that Darras also reported the arrival at the manor of our old friend Carmen Vlaxi.'

'Vlaxi!'*

The whole room was alert now. Vlaxi was well known to them all. Originally from Toulouse, he had been a small-time operator but had got ambitious and moved north to Paris, then unfortunately into their patch. When Tagliatti, one of their already established local gangsters, had been assassinated over a bullion haul, they'd thought Vlaxi was involved, but apparently he'd had nothing to do with it. However, just after Pel and his team had cleared up the case, they'd received a call from Pépé le Cornet, now retired on his ill-found gains and living in luxury in the capital, to say that Vlaxi had taken over Tagliatti's operation. Since then it was true Vlaxi had been very quiet, coming and going from his newly acquired expensive house just outside their city, but at least behaving himself. Now, here he was again, fraternising with their guest of honour, the American Margay. The case grew more and more interesting by the minute, Pel thought. Perhaps Vlaxi merited a short and to-the-point visit, just to let him know they hadn't forgotten him. And perhaps they should find out a bit more about Margay. If Vlaxi was interested in him, so was Pel.

'Perhaps, de Troq', you should quietly try and find out what Margay was doing at this hotel in Montauban. It may be that he was there on legitimate business – it's a big city with a lot of commerce. We are, as I'm sure the Chief would be the first to point out, investigating a break-in at Margay's house, not Margay himself.' He looked up at the Chief, who said nothing. 'However, the fact that Vlaxi paid him a call makes Margay himself all the more interesting.'

Annie Saxe's mop of red hair appeared round the door. 'Phone call, Chief. I've put it through to your office.'

* see Pel and the Picture of Innocence.

Looking harassed, he rose and left Pel and his team to discuss the two murders.

Aimedieu had done his stuff, interviewing all the people connected with the two dead women, including their families, friends, neighbours, even the sightseers who had collected to watch the bodies being removed, but there was no lead as to their murderer or murderess.

'As far as I can ascertain,' Aimedieu pointed out, 'there was no reason for murder that we can find. Madame Marty was an elderly lady living with her bedridden husband. She had little money – in fact, to make ends meet, she occasionally took in a lodger. She's not supposed to because she's in a council flat, but the neighbours said nothing. She was well liked and well respected. No one I spoke to wished her any harm. On the contrary, they were shocked to learn of her death and couldn't offer any suggestions.'

Nosjean tried to interupt, but Pel waved him down, 'Let Aimedieu finish,' he said. 'You're next.'

Aimedieu continued. 'The second woman was quite a different kettle of fish, not very well liked, loud-mouthed, and although we don't know her officially as being on the game, her neighbours all implied that the men who called at the flat were not just friends. They suggested they were clients, but that could just be gossip. She was thirty-five, divorced twice, two children, one by each marriage, the first being born when she was only sixteen, the second when she was eighteen. Both have since left home to live in Dunkirk and Marseilles. They are both married and work in local factories. Although Lulu Lafon talked a great deal about her children, it's been years since they came and visited her. However,' he concluded, 'although no one seemed very fond of her, there were no real enemies. She had a few debts but only small, a hundred francs at the tobacconist, fifty francs at the boulangerie, she owed the old girl downstairs the cost of a bottle of pastis, but apart from that nothing important.

In fact we found a couple of hundred-france notes stuffed under the mattress, but we found no real cause for murder. I've been in touch with her ex-husbands, and they were surprised, saying she was a nag but didn't deserve to be killed for it. This one's a real puzzler.'

Nosjean was, by now, squirming in his seat, looking like a poodle needing to be let out.

'All right,' Pel said, 'It's obvious that you've got something to add. You'd better get on with it before you wet yourself.'

The other policemen chuckled, but Nosjean was not put off. He opened his file, considered for a moment then began.

'I went to see the old boy yesterday,' he started. 'Madame Marty's husband. He was witness to his wife's killing, but not much use we thought, because he's blind, paralysed from the waist down and doesn't speak. However, he's not deaf and spends a lot of time listening to the radio or television. Something he'd heard had set his rusty old mind grinding into action. He'd been agitated ever since the midday news. The nurses thought it was because of the report of his wife's death, but it was more. I got to his bedside late yesterday afternoon. For a while I talked and asked questions but he only managed to gurgle. I couldn't understand a thing, neither could the nurses, then I remembered Darcy's suggestion that he may be able to write. With a bit of help I managed to get a pencil fixed into his right hand and a notepad into the left. He slammed them both down on the bedcovers, gurgling frantically, so we switched them over. He's left-handed, and once we'd established the fact it was only a question of trying to read his terrible handwriting. It wasn't easy, I can tell you.'

By this time Pel was becoming delirious with impatience. 'Get on with it, Nosjean – what in the name of God did he tell you, or write?'

Nosjean was unperturbed and went on calmly. 'He spent a long time scribbling. I left him to it, only turning the pages as he filled each one up. After some time he went limp and the notepad and pencil fell on to the bed. He'd had a minor heart attack and I was removed rapidly from his room. I sat for hours puzzling over his erratic scribbling, but I finally got it.'

'Well?' Pel shot the word across the room at Nosjean like a bullet from a gun.

'He'd written "Italian" then an equals sign and the word 'here'. Look.' Nosjean passed his notepad over. It was hard to decipher, but now that Pel knew what it was he could make it out.

'Is that all?' Pel was irritated to have waited so long for so little.

'No, there's another. That one reads "Italian plus Lulu equals bed". The third reads "Find Italian".'

'So who the hell's this Italian?'

'Exactly.' Nosjean was making Pel suffer. 'After a few more enquiries at neighbours' flats they began to remember a good-looking chap who could have been Italian who came to visit. He was in his late twenties or early thirties, they said. He appears to have been the lodger at Madame Marty's and the lover of Lulu Lafon.'

'At last.' Pel was relieved it was over. If Nosjean tried hard enough he could be as long-winded as Leguyader of Forensics.

'The only trouble is,' Nosjean finished, 'no one's seen this Italian type since before the murders and no one knows where he lives. He comes from down south, not on the coast but somewhere inland near the Pyrenees. That's all I've got. Although the neighbours knew of him, when I reminded them, they don't know much about him.'

Pel sighed. For a moment it had looked as if they had the break they were searching for. Suddenly it had become a dead end again.

'Well, get back to the old boy, and get him writing again.'

'Unfortunately, patron, I can't'.

'Why not?'

'He died. The nurse phoned first thing to tel me.'

'*Génial*. Our one and only witness, handicapped though he was, has just snuffed it. Well, at least try and find out what this Italian's name is – that might rule out a couple of million immigrants.' Police work could be very discouraging at times.

Madame Pel was very surprised to find Sergeant Misset asking to see her in her office above Nanette's. She knew him of old, and knew also something of his reputation for being a bungler. When he explained why he was there and offered his help she was very amused.

Pel, however, when he was told that evening, was not at all amused. 'Holy Mother of God!' he exploded. 'I'll have him back on traffic for this. What in heaven's name made him think you had a lover?' He looked from beneath his spectacles at his attractive wife. 'You haven't, by the way, have you?'

'Dear Pel,' she replied, kissing him gently on the cheek, 'I have enough to cope with with just you. Do you honestly think I'd have the time, even if I wanted to – and I don't.'

Pel sniffed. 'That's what I thought,' he said.

As he thought about it later, a small malicious smile crossed Pel's face. He wouldn't have Misset back on traffic after all. Instead he went to the phone and got Misset's home number from the officer on duty at the Hôtel de Police. Dialling the number, he was relieved to find it was Madame Misset who answered. With all the false concern he could muster, he explained that, while Misset was very brave, and though he did appreciate his loyalty to the department, after the knock on the head two weeks before, and now the stitched wound, while on active duty, he, Pel, as his senior officer, insisted that

Misset stayed at home and rested for at least a week. Madame Misset seemed delighted.

For the first time for ages Pel slept like a baby that night.

He was blissfully unaware that, in a small hamlet not far from Montauban, things had already happened to change and complicate his investigations considerably.

10

Montauban is the *chef-lieu* of the department, sharing
its boundary with the Tarn. The Tarn, Pays de Passion,
blessed with good weather, good food and excellent wine,
is protected on all sides by land mass. Undisturbed by sea
breezes, the temperatures often rise above those of the
rest of the country. In a small valley, well hidden from
the bustle of the market towns, the air was heavy with
the song of the *cigalles* and crickets. A soft burping of
frogs drifted up from the stream below the house where
a young woman stood listening to the baleful cry of an
overhead buzzard that hung on motionless wings like a
suspended mobile. Nature was gently humming but no
human was moving. On the few old houses, scattered over
the hillsides surrounding her, the shutters were tightly
closed against the heat and the still brilliant early evening
sunshine. The locals kept strictly to the shade during July
and August.

It was heart-breakingly peaceful. Kate sighed with
pleasure at the silence.

It didn't last long.

With a sudden flurry of gravel, four bicycles skidded
to a halt in the farmyard in front of her. Her two sons
and their friends had arrived. They were followed by an
extremely noisy and battered van, out of which climbed
an equally noisy and scruffy couple. The Durand family
had arrived for supper.

Pierre, an electrician, was large, very large, built like a buffalo, with a shock of dusty black hair, permanently standing on end as if he'd made a mistake and stuck his fingers in the wrong socket to test it. His wife, Jo-jo, was shaped like a Perrier bottle, slim on top but getting wider and rounder as she went down. Both of them smiled broadly and greeted Kate with the customary kiss on each cheek.

The large wooden table on the terrace was laid in the dwindling daylight and as dusk approached the noise level increased. Unexpectedly, two colleagues with whom Pierre often worked arrived in another battered van, just in time for the second pastis. Inevitably, the table was relaid and they stayed to share the simple meal washed down with good doses of local red wine.

Finally the four children retired to the bedroom to watch the idiot box, where they eventually fell asleep wrapped in each others' bed covers. The table outside remained full with the debris of the meal and voices were raised and happy as Kate went in to brew the coffee.

Going through the kitchen door, however, she was grabbed roughly. A hand was clamped over her mouth. Jesus! A team of big blokes outside, and she couldn't even cry out for help. Her heart was thumping wildly but as her aggressor turned her slowly round to face him she recognised the man asking her to remain silent.

'Georges, what the hell –'

'Kate, I need the keys to your friend's holiday cottage by the river. Don't ask questions, and don't tell a soul. I need to hide.'

'What is it? How on earth did you get in?'

'Never mind how I got in, I've got to get out and fast. I can't tell you why. Please give me the keys. It's just for a few days. Your friend never uses it and I promise to look after the place. Please, I've got to disappear. If you haven't got the keys back in a week, tell Pierre.'

Kate opened her mouth to speak, but Georges put his hand gently over it. 'Please,' he begged.

The incident troubled Kate. Georges was Pierre's younger brother. Pierre and his wife were her good friends – in fact Jo-jo came to the house every day to help with the animals, feeding the poultry, the dog and cats, exercising the two horses with Kate and looking after the children if she had to go out alone.

Kate had learnt to trust them completely. At two o'clock in the morning, when a couple of drunken young peasants came to serenade her, she'd rung Pierre and he'd climbed out of bed to send them packing in no uncertain terms. It had happened only once. The word had spread that, although Kate had no husband, she was protected.

Georges, however, she knew less well. She'd accepted him because he was Pierre's brother. He came and went, often saying very little, occasionally boasting that he was in the money, but that was rare. She had no idea he knew about the riverside cottage, but obviously Pierre had told him and gone to the trouble of showing him how to reach it, because it wasn't easy on foot and absolutely impossible by car.

Why Georges had wanted the keys to the cottage, and why he wanted to hide, puzzled her. Perhaps it was woman trouble – he had a reputation for chasing married women – but it seemed a dramatic way of escaping that sort of problem. Perhaps this time the husband had been a rugby forward armed with a shotgun. Having been told to wait a week before doing anything, she put it all to the back of her mind and tried to stop worrying. Until the following morning.

Setting off early, with her two small sons strapped into the back seat of her ancient Renault 4, to do the weekly shopping in town, she rattled down the driveway and into the country lane to head out of the valley. Noticing she was low on petrol, she turned left towards her local village where, although there were no shops, there was a bar with a single petrol pump outside. Coming down the other side of the hill from her valley she could see the village nestling in the next dip surrounded by its agriculture and occasional plantations of poplars. To the left and right, the vines marched in straight lines over the horizon, and the fields below on the small plain were glowing with the electric yellow of open sunflowers. At the entrance to the little village was a derelict farmhouse sitting in the middle of an already sunburnt field, empty but for a pretty *pigeonnier* and a small helicopter. Helicopter! Both boys leapt against their seat-belts, like small dogs on chains, and strained their necks to see. A helicopter in Itzac was as unusual as the Martians landing; it deserved noting.

At the solitary petrol pump, as the bent-backed bar owner filled her tank, Kate made the usual noises about the weather and the vineyards.

She was ignored. 'Seen the 'copter?' the man said.

'What's it doing her?'

'Some city blokes looking for Pierre's brother, young Georges. They came and asked me, but I don't know where the blighter is. I told them there was no sense looking here, we haven't seen him in months.'

That afternoon, when Jo-jo came to feed the animals, she looked as if she'd been crying. Her usually sparkling eyes were dull and red. She had a livid bruise under one eye.

'It was Pierre,' she said. 'He lost his temper and hit me.'

Kate found it hard to believe, but Jo-jo insisted, so she let the subject drop. After all, it was none of her business; she shouldn't meddle in other people's marital problems. She'd already lived through a few of her own and nosy-parkers never helped. But as the day wore on she became more and more anxious, believing possibly that it

84

had something to do with the men looking for Georges, or Georges himself. Finally she plucked up courage and asked her.

Jo-jo's eyes opened wide. 'How did you know?'

'Just a guess. What's he been up to?'

'I don't know, honestly I don't. This morning two men came to the house and asked to speak to Pierre. He wasn't there of course, he was at work, and I don't know where this week, he could be installing electricity anywhere between Perpignan and Paris, and I told them exactly that. One of them hit me and told me not to be cheeky. Then they started on about Georges. I don't know where he is, I haven't seen him in ages. I told them that too but they didn't believe me and hit me again to jog my memory. But I didn't tell them anything more. I wouldn't have, even if I'd known,' she added defiantly.

Whether she liked it or not now it was Kate's business. She knew where Georges was even if she didn't know why. She couldn't wait any longer, something had to be done.

When Pierre arrived home that evening, he found the scribbled note Kate had left him and appeared in the farmyard not long after seven o'clock. Over a *coup de blanc* in the kitchen the recent events were calmly explained to him: Georges begging for the keys to the cottage, the helicopter in the village, and finally what had happened to Jo-jo's cheek.

After comforting his wife and shooing the four boys back out into the yard at least a dozen times, he suggested to Kate that they should pay his brother a visit down by the river.

'But it'll be dark soon.' Jo-jo was obviously still frightened by the day's events and didn't want to be left alone that night.

'We'll go tomorrow,' Pierre said, putting his hand over his wife's. 'Although there's still quite a few hours before night falls I think perhaps you're right – there isn't enough time to cross the forest and return in daylight.'

Early the following morning Jo-jo watched them saddle up the two horses, Bebel and Jess, while organising the children into a painting competition. More paint was landing on them than on the large sheets of paper laid out on the terrace, but they were happy and didn't bother to look up as the two riders walked quietly out of the yard.

When Kate had been told, on her arrival in the Tarn, that France has the largest number of hectares of forestland out of all the Common Market Countries, she'd found it easier to believe than most, because one of the things that had pleased her about the house she bought was the forest behind it. It was the size of Paris, and just as tricky. For the most part the trees were oaks, making it dark, dense and intriguing. There was a maze of pathways through it to which the intelligent visitor stuck like glue. Away from the tracks the trees swallowed you up, making it dangerously difficult to find your way out. A few never had. Pierre, however, knew it well, having lived alongside it most of his adult life, and Kate was beginning to know it, having carefully explored its mysterious routes day by day on horseback. They were happy in amongst the vast oak trees and confidently crossed its dark interior towards the Aveyron River on the other side.

The moment they entered the shade of the trees the heat from the blazing sun was cut as if a gas fire had been turned off, and they were surrounded by cool undergrowth and whispering branches which swayed gently as they reached up to the light so far above their heads. It was refreshing and exhilarating, riding in silence, galloping where the track allowed, walking one behind the other where the foliage was too dense or too difficult. They watched constantly for wild boar, one of the natural inhabitants of the forest. Although they were not usually dangerous, it was as wise to be on the look-out: the males could be the size of a small pony and a great deal heavier, and when charging to protect their females could do an enormous amount of damage. A startled deer clattered off through the trees as they approached its grazing ground, to be joined by a stag a little further away. There were no people, it wasn't the hunting season, and the few tourists that went into the trees out of the blistering sun never ventured into the heart of the forest.

Emerging, eventually, on the other side, they could see the river glinting in the sunlight below. Although they were still under a canopy of branches, the heat rose up the hillside like a desert wind. The descent into the river's valley was a difficult and dangerous ride, so dismounting they led the horses single file, finally attaching them to a tree just above the roof-top of the little cottage where Georges was hiding. From there it was a short scramble though the bushes into what masqueraded as a garden. It was overgrown and silent. The tiny cottage was locked and empty. Georges had gone.

'He's been here though,' Kate said, looking at the unwashed plates and unmade bed.

Pierre picked up a pair of binoculars from the small kitchen table. 'These are his,' he said.

'What did he need those for? He's no bird watcher.'

Pierre took the binoculars outside and peered through them like a pirate scanning the horizon, searching for something, perhaps on the opposite bank of the wide river, that could have interested his brother. He saw nothing but a semi-derelict house which had been empty for years.

'Nothing,' he said, 'not a thing worth looking at.'

But Pierre was puzzled. He knew that if his brother had, even in his haste to disappear, remembered to bring with him a pair of binoculars, it was not just because he was sentimentally attached to them.

'I'm staying,' he told Kate. 'I'll bring Jess down and tether her in the garden. I'm going to watch tonight.'

'What on earth for?'

'I don't know. Some things move at night that are still during the day. Just one night. Tell Jo-jo I'll be back first thing in the morning. Perhaps, if she's frightened, she could stay at your place?' ·

Kate agreed. She showed him where the small freezer was, stocked with enough emergency rations for a small army, and after extricating a bottle of wine from the cobwebs in the cellar, she left to do the return journey alone.

Jo-jo was already working herself into a state by the time Pierre returned the next day. She'd been back to her own house briefly to find it had been ransacked. Kate telephoned the bar in the village to find out if the helicopter was still there, but it had gone.

When Pierre rode in, looking like Buffalo Bill arriving to tell them the Indians were coming, both women were worried. It was all they could do to keep their tempers with the children who, permanently bouncing, were unaware of their anxiety.

'Something's not right,' he said, swinging down from the saddle. 'There was movement at that house opposite last night – that's what Georges was watching, I'd like to bet. This morning when daylight came I noticed that the place is still pretending to be a ruin, but in fact part of the roof has been redone, and some of the rotten shutters have been replaced. Last night someone arrived in a van. I couldn't see a thing, but I'm sure there were two or more of them. They went into the house and stayed there more than an hour. Then they left. I think we ought to find out who owns that place, and what's going on there.'

Jo-jo told Pierre of their home being turned inside out.

'I don't like the smell of this,' he said. 'Georges has been up to something he's not telling me. I've got a feeling that it's going to be bigger trouble than he expects.'

Not far from where they lived was a scruffy farmhouse surrounded by a few hectares of scruffy vineyards. The chicken, the dogs, the vegetable garden, everything about the dwelling was scruffy, including the two peasants who lived side by side in the house. Old and nosy, they spent every free moment gossiping or listening. They knew everything about everyone, and what they didn't know they made up. It was to these two old men that Pierre went to find out the name of the owner of the house across the river.

They knew the house all right. They hunted every day it was legal and fairly regularly when it wasn't. They rarely bagged anything more than a rabbit or two, but for them it was meat. In their hunting they walked miles through the forest and along the river bank. They knew the area and its inhabitants better than anyone. They also knew that the part of the house that had been reroofed and reshuttered was well locked with stout doors and iron bars. They hadn't managed to see a thing inside.

Proudly divulging the owner's name they continued to gossip like two seasoned landladies. Pierre left them to it. The name meant nothing to him. It wasn't local, but he hardly expected that it would be. When he told Kate, however, something stirred in the back of her memory and, going to her boys' large untidy bedroom, she started shovelling out the rubbish from the floor.

At last the postcard surfaced, missing inevitably the pretty foreign stamp that had been added to their collection, but the writing was still legible. She stood reading and re-reading it. It had arrived a number of weeks before, she couldn't remember exactly when, and she had thought

89

the final sentence was a joke or a meaningless puzzle. Now she realised it was a great deal more.

'Cats! You have the missing Links under your nose. If in doubt, tell Pel.'

Pel! Of course!

11

Pel had at last called in Didier Darras. There seemed little point in leaving him on surveillance when nothing was happening at Margay Manor. It had already happened. Furthermore, Vlaxi had paid Margay a visit. That was something else which was of great interest.

The sunshine had baked the ground hard, drying out the streams and worrying the farmers. Didier had had enough of being an artist. The glare of the sunlight gave him a headache and the lack of activity at the manor was less than enthralling. In his boredom he had even tried his hand at painting. The result ended up in the dustbin – it looked as if a dozen ducks had slid across the paper. He was delighted to be called in and he made his way to Pel's office to receive new instructions.

'We're going to see Vlaxi,' Pel announced before Darras had time to ask. 'What do you know about him?'

'Christian name, Carmen, half Spanish, half Arab. Started business in Toulouse until he moved north. Pretends to be Castilian. Took over what was left of Maurice Tagliatti's operation after he was killed. Used to live in Paris, recently moved to Burgundy. So far we haven't been able to pin anything on him.'

'Congratulations!' Pel looked genuinely surprised. 'You've done your homework well.'

'When I reported Vlaxi's visit to Margay Manor,' Darras

explained, 'I had the impression I'd caused a minor sensation, so I thought I'd better find out why.'

'And now,' Pel said, 'you're going to meet the man himself.'

Vlaxi's house was to the south-east of the city on the edge of a village called Neuilly-les-Dijon. It was a good solid *maison de maître*, with a collection of balconies and white-painted shutters pulled to against the sun. Set well back from the road, it had long green lawns stretching out in front of it. Pel had only ever seen lawns like that in England and wondered how the hell Vlaxi managed it when every other scrap of grass in the gardens around was already turning brown. Then he noticed a fine mist over the whole garden. Realising Vlaxi had installed underground sprinklers, Pel eyed it with suspicion. Anyone who could afford that sort of thing must be up to no good. The house itself wasn't as big as Margay Manor, but it was big enough, with large wrought-iron gates at the entrance. They were firmly locked.

Pel, having never liked gadgets, got Darras to work the intercom system and shortly afterwards there was a click as the gates were unlocked electronically. As they made their way towards the front door a hefty man came out to receive them. He had a face like an all-in wrestler and a voice to go with it, deep and grating as if his throat was full of gravel, but he politely told them that Vlaxi was in residence and waiting to see them in the library.

Library! Pel wondered if anyone in the house could actually read. Vlaxi, when he'd met him the first and only time, had sported horn-rimmed spectacles and an innocent intellectual expression which made him look like a professor of physics, but that didn't mean a thing.

The library was a large circular room, having been converted from the only tower at one corner of the house. Its walls were lined with leather-bound books, every one of them in perfect condition; Pel was sure that none of them had ever been opened, if indeed they were books at all.

They could well be cardboard cut-outs just there to look pretty, or hiding safes containing devious plans, or even a door to a secret escape route. Anything was possible in Vlaxi's world.

Vlaxi was seated behind an impressive desk, its top also bound in leather. He was a handsome little devil, built like a torero and perfectly tanned to an even honey-brown. His immaculately cut dark brown hair was carefully swept across the top of his head from a side parting, hiding, Pel hoped, a growing bald patch. Pel had no such problems – his hair, sparse for a long time, lay across his head like wet seaweed on a rock. Vlaxi's black Arab eyes didn't waver beneath long thick lashes, lashes that any woman would have been proud of, but the eyes were cold and black, sharp as knives, even behind his glasses. Pel liked him less than the first time he'd seen him in Paris.

He had a number of papers in front of him at which he now glanced. He made no sign of realising Pel and Didier were there until the all-in wrestler coughed loudly. Vlaxi sprang to life as if he'd been rehearsing it all morning.

'Ah, Inspector Pel.'

Pel glared. 'Chief Inspector,' he corrected.

'Of course. Excuse me, I was in the middle of some important calculations. I like to play the stock market you know, but the Paris Bourse is not being very helpful today.'

Pel raised his eyebrows. He'd never felt he had enough money to bet on the dogs, let alone the stock market.

'I didn't notice you arrive,' Vlaxi went on. 'Please sit down and make yourselves comfortable.'

The all-in wrestler provided the policemen with a matching pair of leather-bound chairs and withdrew to put his back against the door, presumably, Pel thought, to stop them escaping had they had the inclination. They sat in front of Vlaxi like two schoolboys called to the headmaster's study.

'Can I offer you a drink? Non-alcoholic, of course –

I don't indulge and neither do my staff. But we have grapefruit juice or *grenadine syrop*, even Coca Cola if you prefer.'

Pel declined them all, preferring to rummage in his pocket and produce a crumpled packet of Gauloises, but as he lifted the much-needed cigarette to his lips the infuriating Vlaxi raised a hand. 'No smoking, please. I don't smoke –'

'Yes, let me guess, and neither do your staff.' Pel finished the sentence for him and removed the cigarette with a sweep of his hand, irritated at being forced to abstain. What the hell *did* this man do? he wondered, apart from being a crook of course, that much was obvious.

'So,' Vlaxi said, leaning back in his chair, 'to what do I owe this honour?'

'I just thought you'd like to know we're keeping our eyes on you,' Pel replied. 'You've only just arrived in the area and it occurred to me that it could be helpful to see what our new villain's set-up looks like.'

'Now, Inspector –'

'Chief Inspector,' Pel growled.

'Yes, indeed.' Vlaxi wasn't the slightest bit put off, however. 'Are you accusing me of doing something unlawful? If that's the case, I think I should have my legal consultant present.'

'I'm not accusing you of anything,' Pel said. 'Yet,' he added for good measure. 'But it has come to my notice that you visited Monsieur Margay recently. As you may know, he was robbed not long ago and I had an idea you may be able to help me with my enquiries.'

'I'm going to have to disappoint you, Chief Inspector. The visit was purely social. I'm having a party, to introduce myself to the local dignitaries. Naturally, I've invited everyone who's anyone in the district, and Margay looks like becoming someone round here. After all, everyone's talking about him. Unfortunately, he's a snob and has

94

refused to come. A shame,' he finished. 'We could have done business together.'

He said it so naturally that Pel was inclined to believe him. However, he wasn't completely convinced. 'When's this party of yours to be held?'

'Bastille Day, July the fourteenth, seemed as good a date as any.' Vlaxi looked self-satisfied as he smiled across the desk at them. 'I'll see to it that you receive a formal invitation, if you like,' he added.

'Don't bother. I shan't be coming either.'

'Another shame – we ought to try and be hospitable towards one another, to our mutual advantage, of course.'

Hospitable to an oily villain like Vlaxi, never! He was a tricky customer, too smooth by half and far too virtuous. No booze, no cigarettes, what in the name of God made the bloke tick? Apart from the stock exchange, and Pel didn't believe that was all for a moment. It was far more likely that he had been studying a list of the misdemeanours of his guests and was calculating the possible profits from a nice line in blackmail. Pel decided it would be very interesting to see who turned up at his party. As it was a national holiday, the surveillance wouldn't go down too well – but that was part of being a policeman. To his surprise Didier Darras had had the same idea and volunteered to be in the bushes outside Vlaxi's house on the night of the fourteenth.

'The man's a weasel,' he explained in the car on their way back. 'Now I've got a vague idea of the layout of the place I'd like to see what goes on.'

It wasn't what any of them expected.

12

Pel was sitting in the Chief's office when the phone rang. The Chief answered it and handed the receiver to Pel.

'It's for you.'

'There's a lady asking for you, patron. She insists on speaking to you personally. Her name, by the way, is Lady Smythe.'

Pel sighed. He'd never heard of her. 'You'd better put her through,' he said.

'*Pel à l'appareil*,' he announced when the clicking of the extension finished its little serenade.

'Chief Inspector Pel, I'm very sorry to disturb you. I do appreciate how busy you must be.' The voice was smooth and educated, and although the name had been utterly English, there was no trace of an accent. She spoke perfect French; he hoped it was going to be worth listening to. 'I had to insist on speaking to you, those were my instructions. The fact is, monsieur, I have a story to tell you. Would it be possible for us to meet?'

Pel had a feeling that it would probably be his pleasure, but his ankle was still agony in spite of his wife's loving care and, besides, he had a great deal on his plate with Margay's robbery and two murders.

'I do understand,' she continued, 'that being so far away it will be inconvenient, but it's important and possibly urgent.'

Pel definitely didn't have the time to go galloping all

over the country, even to please aristocratic ladies with charming voices.

'Couldn't you give me the details over the phone?' he asked.

'I'd rather not,' came the reply. 'The story is quite a long one. If you can't come yourself,' she suggested, 'I'd be very happy to see one of your inspectors, Darcy, de Troquereau or Nosjean.'

Pel was slightly surprised that the lady knew of them. How the hell had she got that information if she lived so far away?

'From where did you get their names?'

'Chief Inspector, I'll be happy to explain all that when I see someone. But', the lady was becoming agitated, 'I must see someone, and quickly.'

Pel considered rapidly. 'Where exactly are you?' he asked.

'Midi-Pyrénées, just north of Toulouse.'

It was nearly a day's drive away. It would have to be de Troq'. Nosjean was too busy with the murder investigations and Darcy had disappeared off the face of the earth.

'D'accord,' he said eventually. 'I'll send de Troq' to hear your story. I hope it's a good one.'

'It is, Chief Inspector. You won't be disappointed.'

'Very well. He won't be available until tomorrow at the earliest. In the mean time, you'd better give me your exact address.'

It was a slightly irritated Pel who put the phone down. Pleasant though she had sounded, she was obviously the same as all aristocrats – thought she could get away with anything just because she had a title. He was a policeman, an overworked one at that, not a Russian spy. He wondered for a moment why he had agreed to send de Troq', but it was done now. He'd have to wait and see what this mysterious story turned out to be.

Holy Mother of God! he thought. Americans, dead

bodies by the lorry load, cryptic messages from Hong Kong, and now titled ladies requesting clandestine meetings with his officers! What was his beloved Burgundy coming to?

'De Troq', he bellowed, passing his office, 'come and see me. At once.'

But it was Annie Saxe, the Lion of Belfort, who appeared before him. Arriving at speed, full of enthusiasm, she nearly collided with Pel who was taking a gentle stroll round his desk with a file in his hand.

'Not in, sir,' she announced.

'Find him.'

'Yes, sir.'

'And Annie . . .' Pel looked up from the papers he was studying. 'Try and do it without knocking anyone over.' He treated her to one of his rare humorous smiles and succeeded in looking worse than ever.

Annie backed out of the office at more than her usual remarkable speed.

It was quite late that afternoon when Pel's troops started making their way back to the Hôtel de Police. Margay's robbery, with the list of workmen, and the two murders, with all the neighbours and families, were taking up all the hours and more that a normal working day held. Everyone had to be followed up and questioned, and each one of his team was out on the streets doing just that. While sometimes, though not often, they were lucky and a villain made a mistake, leaving them a clue which made their lives much easier and the arrests far quicker, usually it was a matter of long hours of tramping the streets and questioning, making reports and comparing what every cop had found out. Eventually, a pattern or a common denominator would emerge. Invariably it wasn't what they had expected, but it gave them a signpost to point them in the right direction to solve a case. A lot of police work was very tedious, but that's what, in the end, brought results.

As the Sergeants' Room began filling up, the men compared their notes and laboriously typed out their reports with two fingers on old machines discarded from the typing pool. Nothing earth-shattering had come to light for the moment, and they were feeling decidedly uninspired. The heat of the day had exhausted all of them. Most sensible Frenchmen stayed behind closed shutters between midday and two o'clock, only venturing out to return to their place of work, mercifully usually an air-conditioned office block. The peasants didn't bother putting their heads outside again until at least four o'clock, when the heat was beginning to subside. They preferred to have a short *sieste* during the afternoon and catch up in the fields and vineyards during the evening. This, however, was not the case for the police. Their lunch was a snatched sandwich in between making their enquiries, and in this heat it was soul-destroying.

Annie Saxe had the bright idea of going across the road to the Bar Transvaal and bringing back a dozen cold beers. The returning men fell on them as if they'd come in from crossing the Sahara. She was also bright enough to take one in to Pel.

'De Troq's not yet reported in,' she said as she placed the frosted bottle and clean glass on his desk. 'I'll send him along as soon as he arrives.'

She was gone before Pel could reply. That girl is learning fast, he thought, and reached out to quench his thirst.

He was finishing the last of his beer when de Troq' appeared in his office holding a half-empty glass.

'Good idea of Annie's. It went down well in the Sergeants' Room.'

'It shouldn't happen every day,' Pel replied with a mild display of authority. 'By the way, what do you think of her?'

99

'She's no fool.'

That was exactly what Pel thought.

'I've got a new assignment for you, de Troq'. Hand over all you've got to Nosjean. I know he's dealing with the two murders, but if he delegates and uses the men you've had up till now, he should be able to cope with the robbery as well. You're going on a trip.' He handed him the address.

'That's quite a way. When do I leave?'

'Tomorrow morning. The faster you leave the faster you'll be back.'

The Hôtel de Police had gone quiet. It was after nine o'clock and only the skeleton staff remained. And de Troq' and Nosjean. A dozen reports had been typed out that evening and, being responsible for the investigations, they had to go through every one from their own teams, checking for new developments. Later de Troq' went through each one from his team again with Nosjean. He was handing over the Margay case and often it was helpful to go over the information together rather than just read other men's reports. This way they learnt personal opinions and feelings, things that didn't appear in a report, which dealt only with facts.

De Troq' had for days now been following up the workmen involved in the renovations at Margay Manor. He'd managed to rule them all out with one exception, but even he was a dubious suspect.

'Bargiacchi,' he said, referring to his notes. 'Giorgio Bargiacchi. Twenty-five, mother's dead, father of unknown address. Giorgio has no record, but his father has. It took some digging to find the details, but through the records at Nantes headquarters I finally turned up his parents. His father did time for a number of robberies, plus beating up the partner that shopped him. He sounds like a nasty piece of work. Unfortunately

100

the bloke's disappeared. It was a long time ago but it showed up loud and clear in the end. We have no current address for either father or son, but it would be worth looking up his brother Giuseppe, who was last heard of in Montauban.'

But Nosjean was no longer paying attention. He was flicking through his own file of reports. He extricated a sheet of paper and handed it to de Troq'. For a moment Nosjean and de Troq' stared at each other.

'The Italian!'

As de Troq' was already due to leave for the Midi-Pyrénées the following morning it was decided that he should, on his way through, call in at Montauban and look up Giuseppe.

It had been a long and tiring drive, most of it on what was known as the Sunshine Motorway leading from Paris to the coast. Fortunately the first rush of holiday-makers was over, but it was a long way all the same before, turning right towards Carcassonne and Toulouse, he at last left the motorway and headed for Montauban.

The market town was a buzz of activity, and although the Préfecture de Police was well signed on entering the city, he found, as is often the case, a distinct lack of directions immediately afterwards. However, more by luck than judgement, he finally drew up outside the Préfecture. It was an impressive building, a renovated château with magnificent grounds, but unfortunately spoilt by a monstrous modern office block in the front garden. De Troq' wasted no time on sightseeing, but headed straight for the information desk in the new building.

He left less than an hour later, disappointed. Their records showed that Giuseppe Bargiacchi was no longer in the area but had moved to the next *canton*. Pel was disappointed too. After their discovery the previous

101

evening he'd hoped that this was going to be the break they'd all been waiting for.

'Keep digging,' he told de Troq' when he phoned in late that afternoon. 'Try the gendarmaries, Securité Sociale, the Employment Office, the local prison, everyone. We've got to find this Bargiacchi, and he was last heard of down there. You've got to turn something up.'

What he turned up, however, was not quite what he'd anticipated.

It was Darcy.

13

The only lead de Troq' had to work on was Bargiacchi's brother. He'd been told that he'd moved into the next *département*, the Tarn. His attempts to trace him had led him to the head town of the *canton*, and it was there in Albi that he came face to face with his colleague from Burgundy.

'What the hell are you doing here?'

Darcy looked equally surprised at finding his fellow inspector, de Troquereau, lurking in the corridors of the Préfecture in Albi. 'I could ask you the same question,' he said.

'I'm here to see a lady,' de Troq' replied.

'So am I. What's the name you've got?'

'Lady Smythe.'

Darcy smiled his crooked smile. 'You've always been a snob about titles,' he said. 'I've got the very ordinary Cathérine Henri.'

Both men had finished their business amongst the records of the Préfecture, fiddling their way through thousands of applications for *cartes de séjour*, small pieces of plastic, like credit cards, issued to foreigners making it lawful for them to stay in France. In 1992, it had been said, with the advent of Europe, the system would be abolished, but it had taken a little longer and for the time being it was a very convenient way of keeping tabs on the immigrants in any given area.

Darcy had successfully unearthed Cathérine Henri's address, and although de Troq' already had that of Lady Smythe, given to him by Pel, he hadn't found anything for Bargiacchi. That meant going through the massive lists at Securité Sociale. He wasn't looking forward to it and readily agreed to join Darcy for lunch. The offices of Securité Sociale would be closed between midday and two o'clock anyway. It gave them a small breathing space.

They crossed the busy road to head for the Café Pontié on the corner of the main square. Cars were racing past in their thousands, squealing to a halt at the red traffic lights and as they turned to green shrieking away again as if it was the start of the Monaco Grand Prix. The two police-men installed themselves at a table on the pavement just before midday, to watch the whirlpool of vehicles as battle commenced for going home at lunchtime. The café was nearly empty when they arrived, but within half an hour there wasn't a table free. Although Albi had the biggest *lycée* in the Tarn there were no youngsters at the bar, with its Parisian-style décor and magnificent chandelier. The Pontié attracted Albi's businessmen and their smart little secretaries, the accountants and dentists, who stayed in the city to eat. As at most enterprising cafés, there was a simple menu at lunchtime, consisting of salads, the usual *steack-frites*, and the inevitable sandwiches made from steel-crusted baguettes that lacerated your gums, and filled with either a piece of plastic ham or rubber pâté. De Troq' and Darcy had to admit, however, that it was clean and better than most, and at least the wine didn't taste as if it had metal fatigue.

As they finished eating, de Troq' produced the local map he'd acquired to compare notes on where they were both headed. Darcy had arrived the evening before by T.A.T. airlines from Paris, touching down in a small jet at Albi's motor-racing circuit – this doubled up as an airport when there was no meeting in progress, which was most of the time. He therefore had no car and was hoping that de Troq' might just be going in the direction of Cathérine Henri. He'd had a good look at the maps on the walls at the Préfecture and made one or two enquiries. The address he had was fifteen kilometres from the nearest bus stop, which meant he would have to hire a car, a lengthy and extremely expensive business.

De Troq' pointed to the name Itzac. 'That's where I'm going,' he said. 'Or at least not far from there.'

'Itzac, Shitzac and all the other bloody Zacs,' Darcy mused. 'There are a lot of them about. Hang on.' He sat up and studied the map more carefully. 'But that's where I'm headed.'

Darcy had forgotten how beautiful Albi was, and in trying to find their way out of the city they passed in front of the magnificent cathedral of Saint Cécile, built in the thirteenth century in remarkably small red bricks.

'Bishop Bernard de Castenet', de Troq' informed him, 'started the building, and when it was finished a fleet of Italian artists were brought in during the sixteenth century to paint the inside with frescos.'

'Right up and over the vaulted ceilings,' Darcy added. 'I don't remember much, there were too many pretty girl tourists about when my grandparents brought me here, but I do remember tearing my eyes away from them long enough to look at the paintings and found them somewhat awe-inspiring.'

'The great organs are the work of Christophe Moucherel of Toulouse,' de Troq' went on, 'finally installed between 1734 and 1736.'

'You do carry a lot of useless information around in your head,' Darcy, laughed. 'Where do you get it all from?'

'My family and my education. As I was one of the de Troquereau de Turennes, the history of France was part of my childhood – in fact, I was saturated in it from the moment I was born. It doesn't help a great deal with

105

police work, I must confess,' he smiled, 'but it enriches my travelling from time to time.'

'So what do you know about Toulouse-Lautrec?' The story of the famous painter was one thing that had stuck firmly in Darcy's mind even through all his adolescent flirtings.

'He fell off his chair when he was fourteen and again when he was fifteen, breaking first his left then his right thighbones which crippled him for the rest of his life.'

'That was bloody careless,' Darcy said, startled. 'I thought it was because his parents were cousins that he was stunted.'

'Indirectly it must have been – because of the frailty in his genes, he developed a disease in his bones and the breaks never healed properly, hence he remained a dwarf for the rest of his life.'

'Poor miserable old sod.'

'But he wasn't. He was a charming man, cheerful even. You've only to look at his posters and pictures to see his *joie de vivre*. No one could have painted so much vitality and laughter if he'd been miserable.'

Darcy was beginning to wish he'd paid more attention when he'd visited the permanent exhibition next to the cathedral, but it was too late now and they were already heading out into the countryside. Toulouse-Lautrec would have to wait for another day to be given his full attention, one day when he was less busy. Perhaps after he retired, he'd come back and have a second look.

On the straight road that left the city, de Troq' stopped to put down the hood of his battleship-sized roadster. Shortly afterwards they found their way on to a small country road in the direction of Itzac. It was still some way but in the intense heat of the early afternoon it was a pleasure to feel the breeze on their faces. They wound their way through endless vineyards, covering the softly undulating countryside, scattering chickens and disturbing the occasional sleepy mongrel dog stretched out in the middle of a narrow village street. Not a soul was out of doors; away from the bustle and air-conditioning of the city, nothing but the dust stirred on the lonely twisting lanes. Shutters were closed, *sieste* was in force.

Darcy had Coste as the name of the house where Cathérine Henri lived; de Troq' had Château Coste, naturally. They had assumed it would be a small hamlet in the shadow of the one and only decent dwelling, the château. It was also possible, however, that the village and the château were miles apart. It was a coincidence all the same.

As they arrived at the village of Itzac, de Troq' pulled the car to a stop in front of the bar so that they could refresh themselves and ask for directions to Coste and the château.

The bent barman was less than enthusiastic. 'Right round the *pigeonnier*, and the twits that are always there painting it, right again, follow the bends in the road till you come to a junction. Left, then right, left again and into the valley. You'll see it on the hillside above you then.'

'Coste or the château?'

'Same thing.' The barman sighed, turning his back on them to wipe the counter. 'Or at least it has been ever since I've been here, which is sixty-two years.' He dismissed them with a shrug. 'You'll find it, it's signed, certainly was the last time I looked.'

It was a small château, more like an overgrown farmhouse, with a pair of towers and a number of outbuildings surrounding a courtyard. It was built in local pale stone and topped by pink and beige *terre cuite* roofing tiles, sitting on the side of the valley in full sunshine, almost as if it were spotlit. At the entrance to the driveway were two massive oak trees; the girth of their huge trunks and the vast pools of shade over the broken-down gates suggested to de Troq' that they must have been planted during the Revolution, as many were. Above and below the buildings, the vineyards stretched in all directions. From a distance

107

it had looked peaceful and welcoming. Closer, it looked much shabbier. It was quite obviously inhabited – a string of washing hanging limply in the breathless heat told them that – but most of the château consisted merely of barns, the majority of them in need of attention. As they drove under the archway into the courtyard the car sent a cloud of doves into the air. The yard was crowded with chickens, guinea fowl and a string of ducks making their way in a tidy column towards a small pond in one corner. Propped beside the pond was a tall ladder at the top of which was perched, like the now reposing doves, a young lad splashing paint on to a delapidated shutter. On the other side of the yard, stretched out in the sunshine, was an enormous black dog being used as a pillow by a number of cats of assorted colours. There were also a number of small boys tearing round the yard on bicycles, unperturbed by the searing heat. As he whizzed past, one of them shouted to the strangers in the large car, 'Don't get out, the dog'll eat you. All we have to do is shout "Attack!"'

They looked again at the dog. It hadn't made a move. However, when Darcy opened his door and put an exploratory foot to the ground, the black beast rose to his feet showering the cats like confetti. He was as big as a sideboard and just as solid, but when he curled back his lips in a snarl they could see his teeth were far from being wooden. Darcy withdrew his foot and slammed the door shut quickly.

The lad who had been painting the shutters had come down the ladder and was making his way across the yard towards the car. He was wearing blue overalls well splattered with paint and a peaked cap equally well decorated. He stopped some way from them. He was still in shadow, and they were unable to see his face.

'What do you want?'

Darcy presented himself, flipping out for good measure

his badge showing the red, white and blue stripes of the police.

'And your identity card,' the lad demanded, looking at de Troq'. He too offered his card for consultation.

'Okay, so you're policemen. I knew you were on your way – the barman phoned and told me. What do you want?'

'I wouldn't mind stretching my legs without losing one to your dog, if you can get it to calm down.'

'The dog'll calm down when I tell him to, which will be after you tell me what or who you're looking for.'

Darcy sighed. 'I'm looking for Cathérine Henri, known as Kate, daughter of Professor Frédéric Henri, and my colleague is looking for Lady Smythe, mysterious phone caller to Chief Inspector Pel.'

The Tour de France which had been in progress round and round the yard had now come to a halt and four small hostile faces were staring at the two detectives. The dog was simply licking his lips.

'Oh, well, that's all right then,' the lad said suddenly. He put two fingers to his mouth and whistled for the dog to come to heel. 'It's all right, he won't bite you now. You can get out of the car.'

The Tour de France asked permission to go paddling in the stream at the bottom of the drive. Permission was granted by the lad who, stepping into the sunlight and removing his peaked hat, let a mass of black wavy hair fall about her shoulders.

'I'm Kate,' she announced, beaming at them. She was an attractive young woman with large dark eyes and a full smiling mouth. 'I'm also, or was, Lady Smythe. That's how I knew you had to be genuine. I never use that silly title now, but when I phoned Pel it was the only way I could get to speak to him personally. You have a very efficient young lady manning your switchboard.'

Annie Saxe!

'You look parched,' Kate went on cheerfully. 'Come into the kitchen. I could do with a drink myself.'

The monster dog had gone back to his position and was lolling by the side of the house, so all they had to do was ease their way past him through the door and into the safety of the interior.

While the outside of the building was in need of care and attention, the inside was completely renovated. It was spotlessly clean and attractive. The kitchen was immense with various cupboards at one end and a fireplace big enough to hold a party in at the other. There was a huge table that stretched almost the entire length of the room, and on to this Kate was emptying the contents of a giant and ancient fridge.

'They're in here somewhere, I just know they are,' she was saying. 'I bought them specially when I knew de Troq' was on his way.' At last the bottles of beer appeared and she bundled the rest of the contents haphazardly back, firmly closing the door with her foot.

'Sorry about the dog,' she said, smiling at them and removing the bottle tops on the edge of the table with an elegant clout of her fist, 'but there's no man about the place and Rasputin is better protection than any alarm system or shotgun. He puts the fear of God into people and there have been a couple of suspicious characters in the village recently.'

14

'But this is ridiculous!' Pel was on the rampage. 'Find me Darcy!'

'But, sir –'

'He can't have disappeared off the face of the earth. Someone must know where he is.'

'Sir –'

'No excuses. I must speak to him.' Pel banged the phone back into its cradle and viciously wrenched a cigarette from the packet on his desk in front of him. It was the end of a wearing day, he thought, studying the glowing tip of his cigarette with no feelings of guilt whatsoever. He deserved to die happy.

Their enquiries in the city were producing nothing. Nothing but swollen feet and frayed tempers, and still his officers spent the blisteringly hot days tramping the streets patiently asking the same questions over and over again. The result had been frustrating. After the initial elation at discovering the Italian's name, Bargiacchi, and his connection between their three major crimes, the trail had gone cold. Giorgio Bargiacchi, installer of air-conditioning to the rich, lodger to old Madame Marty and lover to Lulu Lafon. He was certainly a man who got about a bit. But where the hell had he got to now? Pel inhaled deeply – even his Gauloise wasn't able to soothe his nerves. He had no answers so far; no one knew where the Italian had got to. Pressure was being brought to bear from all directions and they had nothing to offer to keep the powers that be happy. Pel was frustrated. He reached out to light a cigarette and found to his disgust he already had one alight in his mouth. Things were bad. Bargiacchi must be found, he was the missing link they needed. The missing link. That brought him back to Darcy: he seemed to be missing too, and Pel had to admit that without Darcy, his right-hand man, he felt half-dressed. The department was like a strong chain leading from the Chief to Pel, to Darcy, to Nosjean and so on, right on down to the youngest and most inexperienced detective. When any one of them was absent, except Misset of course, the department lost its strength – it was like a machine without oil in the moving parts, it moved badly and was in danger of stalling. Even with Darcy working on a separate enquiry he was necessary to the smooth running of their operations. Where the hell was he? Had he lost his head as well as his teeth and run away from home? Pel was concentrating so hard on working himself into a really good temper that when the phone trilled on his desk he jumped. He snatched it up.

'Yes?' he snapped, putting as much venom into the word as he could muster.

'I'm putting him through, sir.' Annie Saxe was able to cope with Pel and his snake's bite even at this time in the evening.

'Who, in God's name?'

'Darcy, sir. He just called in.' There was a faint trace of amusement in Annie's voice.

There was the usual clicking and whirring from the extension and finally Pel heard Darcy's voice. It was like music to his ears, not that he let it show.

'Mother of God,' he roared, 'where have you been? I thought your brain was registering "faulty" and you'd emigrated or something.'

'I'm down in the Tarn, patron, near Albi. Didn't Misset tell you? I gave him a message a couple of days ago.'

When Darcy finally rang off, Pel had reached boiling point. He had been simmering gently all afternoon but Misset's latest *faux pas* had succeeded in turning up the heat. So, he'd taken a message from Darcy and failed to communicate it. As a result de Troq' had been sent galloping 600 kilometres south to end up in exactly the same place as Darcy. Pel decided he'd ask Yves Pasquier, his young neighbour, more about the new satellite being sent into outer space to monitor Europe's weather. He wondered if by any chance they needed an experimental policeman to see what it was like up there. He would volunteer Misset.

De Troq', however, wasn't complaining about ending up in the same place as Darcy. Kate Henri, an attractive young woman, with a title too, had insisted they stay for a meal. Another couple had turned up, Pierre and Jo-jo Durand, together with the band of children back from the stream, all wet through and extremely muddy. Their clothes were peeled off and they were hosed down naked in the yard. Because of the drought, washing cars had been banned for a long time, but the government hadn't mentioned children and they were shrieking with delight under the icy jet of water. De Troq' had been put in charge of mixing the evening drinks, being the only one to have heard of English summer punch, and Darcy, quietly seething about his partner's infuriating knowledge of things extraordinary, went to help Pierre light a large barbecue. Kate had made an impression on both of them and Darcy realised their swords were drawn, de Troq's being made of gold and inherited from his ancestors, Darcy's bought at the local ironmonger's. Usually Darcy's good looks were enough to win any girl over, but since they'd been badly reshuffled he feared he didn't stand a chance. Aware that he would like a chance with Kate he was even more self-conscious of his broken smile. He suddenly understood why Pel loathed anyone taller, more good-looking or better dressed than himself, which wasn't uncommon; it put him at a disadvantage, and Darcy wasn't used to that. Not that Kate was the most beautiful girl he'd ever seen, not at all. Looking at her surreptitiously from behind the barbecue's wood pile he noticed she was in fact dressed like a peasant in her heavy blue dungarees and clogs, but he also noticed with fascination that there was definitely something about her, something quite different from the polished beauties of the city.

She had attempted to start her story, but had been interrupted so many times by the turbulence of the household that they'd given up and postponed it for after the meal, when at last the children and the poultry would have been put to bed. The guinea fowl doing their impersonation of a rusty well had been the last straw to prevent further sensible conversation.

The dripping youngsters had disappeared inside and for the briefest moment all that could be heard was the crackle of the fire over the gentle belching of the frogs in the stream mingled with the song of the *cigalles*, plus the inevitable guillotining of yards of hard baguette in the kitchen.

The children reappeared, scrubbed, dressed and rosy-cheeked, ready to refilthy themselves in the dusty yard. Kate had gone in, leaving the policemen to wait. There was rivalry between them, although it seemed it was only Darcy who was aware of it; de Troq' was as usual simply self-confident. It was enough to make a man bite the heads off nails. Darcy wasn't racist, but at that moment he would happily have strangled any number of Arabs just for the one who had destroyed his disarming smile.

As Kate reappeared, de Troq' rose and handed her a slim glass of punch with a slice of orange delicately poised on the rim. As she smiled back at him, Darcy realised that she was, after all, one of the most attractive women he'd ever

114

seen. Apparently all she'd done was brush her hair and change her clothes. She wore no make-up, no jewellery, no shoes, preferring to pad quietly barefoot across the terrace, but the simple cotton dress she wore showed all the curves that had been hidden before and had the effect of leaving Darcy slightly breathless. At that moment the wind changed and the smoke from the barbecue swirled round him, reducing him to a violent fit of coughing. He felt that he and Pel were partners: life was well and truly against them.

When they finally got down to business, it was late. The Durands had taken their two boys home to bed, and Kate's sons had, after protesting mildly, also retired. De Troq', Darcy and Kate remained outside in the now cooling evening to enjoy breathing normally after the suffocating heat of the day.

Darcy showed Kate his copy of the strange letter Pel had received from Professor Henri.

'Father likes puzzles,' she said calmly. 'He always said archaeology is a detective story, but this time it seems to have got out of hand. I don't understand why he wanted me to tell Pel.' She handed them her own message from Hong Kong. 'Or why he told Pel to contact the Shrew.'

'Who is the Shrew? It's no one we know.' Darcy wanted an answer to at least one of his questions.

'But you do – it's me. I'm the Shrew.'

Neither of them expected such a simple answer.

'My Christian name is Cathérine,' she explained, 'and like Katharina in Shakespeare's play, *The Taming of the Shrew*, I was always very stubborn, even tempestuous as a youngster, so my father nicknamed me the Shrew.'

De Troq' smiled to himself. He remembered having suggested Shakespeare's character to Pel.

'But it was a very private joke,' she continued. 'Maman didn't encourage it, so why on earth Father expected Pel to work it out I can't imagine.'

'But we found you,' Darcy pointed out.

'Yes, but why?'

'He says you know the missing link.'

'I'm not sure what he means.' She turned both the messages round to face her. 'At first it meant nothing to me at all, then I discovered there is a man in this area called Incks, Charles L. Incks, to be precise, and I wondered if that was what he meant. If you say the name quickly one could mistake the surname for Links.'

'And the warning about cats?'

'Well, a lynx is a wild cat, isn't it, only it's spelt differently, but he's only one. And why beware? Charles L. Incks does own a house by the river, and Georges Durand does seem to have been watching it, but what it all means, I haven't the foggiest idea. Perhaps I'd better start at the beginning and see what you both make of it.'

She told them about Georges' appearance in her kitchen and the events that had taken place since. They sat for a while over a small cognac, trying to work out their puzzle, until they realised with surprise that it was the early hours of the morning and far too late to consider finding an hotel. Kate suggested they sleep in the barn. Expecting to be put to bed with Rasputin, the monster dog, they were inclined to refuse, but she pointed out that upstairs were a couple of rooms with all the essentials for a good night's sleep. They stumbled gratefully up the rickety wood staircase to the converted hay loft, still mystified by her story and the possible connection with what had happened in Burgundy.

How was the Professor involved? What was it in Hong Kong that he'd discovered to make him anxious about cats in France?

15

Pel was in no mood for jokes when he arrived at the Hôtel de Police the following morning. He'd had the bandages taken off his ankle and it had left him limping savagely. Only Pel knew how to limp savagely. Hearing laughter coming from the Sergeants' Room, he slammed open the door to tear a strip off whoever was being frivolous.

There was no need for him to utter a word: a deathly hush fell instantly over all present. He turned on his heel, smiling to himself, satisfied that he could fill most of his team with terror just by looking at them.

The phone was already ringing as he entered his office and it was no surprise to find it was Darcy again. He settled back into his chair to listen carefully. Teeth or no teeth, Darcy's mind was still in top gear.

'There's more to all this than meets the eye,' Pel said eventually. 'Get back to the village and see those two peasants known as Radio Itzac, see if they can tell you any more about this chap Incks. I've heard the name before, I'm sure. While you're doing that tell de Troq' to get over to Montauban and find out what Margay was doing in the hotel there, and whether he was seen with anyone apart from his "boys", Patterson and Goldberg. And tell him to find Bargiacchi – we need him!'

*

There was a definite link between the two murders in the city, but their Italian was still on the loose. De Troq' and Nosjean had discovered that this same man was wanted for questioning with regard to the robbery at Margay Manor, which meant the three events were tied together somehow, one leading on from the other.

'Could Bargiacchi have got away with something more precious than copied treasures?' Nosjean had suggested. 'He seems to be involved in everything that's happening around here at the moment.'

'And down there,' Pel added. 'De Troq' has turned up the Bargiacchi family, apparently now in the Albi area, but he can't lay his hands on them. Where the hell does this bloke Durand come into it? Georges Durand, he's not known to us, is he?'

'Nothing on him as far as we can find. Perhaps he was the second man in the robbery. There's some sort of connection in that area – after all, Margay was in Montauban when the Guardian, Barrau, called him back because of the robbery.'

'Although he was supposed to be on the coast.'

'And the robbery wasn't reported to us until the following morning even though it was urgent enough for Margay to arrive by helicopter the evening before.'

'By then Bargiacchi had disappeared. Bargiacchi, lodger of Madame Marty, now dead, lover of Lulu Lafon, also now dead, and workman at Margay Manor.' Pel turned the facts over in his mind while reaching for another cigarette, hoping his lungs weren't keeping count of how many he'd already smoked that day. 'The house opposite the riverside cottage', he said, 'is owned by an Englishman called Charles L. Incks, which brings us to Professor Henri's strange messages, both to me and to his daughter, about missing links. It's like a bloody jigsaw puzzle with half the pieces missing.'

'Well, at least we know now who the Shrew is,' Nosjean pointed out helpfully.

'Yes, but a fat lot of good it's done us. Where does she fit into all this?'

'Perhaps she doesn't. Perhaps she just happens to be in the right place. Somewhere between Albi and Montauban.'

It was a possibility, but it still didn't help much.

Before he left the office, Pel mustered all his courage together and telephoned his old friend Inspector Goschen in London. They'd worked together on a number of occasions, even visiting each other's homes to be admired by various members of their families.

With his best English, he got through to Scotland Yard and asked to speak to Goschen. To his surprise Goschen seemed delighted to hear Pel's voice. It was always a surprise when someone was delighted to speak to him: he wouldn't have given himself house room.

Between them, with Pel's passable English and Goschen's smattering of French, they made themselves understood.

'Charles L. Incks, yes, I know the name,' Goschen told him, 'but I don't know much about him. Leave it with me for twenty-four hours and I'll get back to you. By the way,' he ended, 'what's the weather like over in France? It's hot in England.'

'Boiling,' Pel retorted, determined not to be outdone by English sunshine. 'Wonderful if you're streamlined and air-conditioned. Unfortunately, I'm neither.'

Pel's final call of the day was to Cousin Roger, the one and only member of his wife's vast family that he got on well with. He was an accountant in the city and had more than once given Pel snippets of useful information. This time he wanted to know something more about their American, Margay. Unfortunately, Cousin Roger, although he'd heard of him – who hadn't? – was unable to tell Pel any more than he knew already, but he rang off with the promise to keep his ear to the

119

ground and an invitation for Sunday lunch in the not too distant future.

Pel was deep in thought as he drove home that evening, mulling over what they already knew, and everything they'd like to know but couldn't find out for the moment. As he swerved and narrowly missed an oncoming car, making his thinning hair stand on end with fright, he made a mental note to tell his wife about the proposed invitation, and to concentrate harder on the road while he was behind the steering wheel.

He arrived at his house wondering whether perhaps a new car would help improve his driving. He didn't seriously think it would, but Madame had been dropping hints for some time now, and although she wasn't in fear of being dumped on the side of the road every time he rounded a corner, as she had been with his last car, it was perhaps time for a change.

Madame was thrilled. Not only a forthcoming invitation to Chaos Corner to see Cousin Roger and his wife, not to mention the four children and uncountable cats and dogs – it was always a very animated household – but also the prospect of a new car. However, she put the fear of God into Pel by suggesting a Mercedes or a BMW.

'What's wrong with French cars?' he replied, looking startled.

Madame soothed her ruffled husband. She knew how to handle Pel. 'Nothing,' she said silkily, 'but I thought it was time to change our image.'

Pel, however, didn't feel the need to change his image in the slightest. He knew he was cantankerous and difficult sometimes, and managed to strike fear into the hearts of the majority of the policemen as well as the criminals of Burgundy – but change his image!

'After all,' his wife was saying, 'we've been married quite some time now.' Indeed, they had. Pel realised what a lucky man he was. 'We can well afford it, business is thriving, we can spend a bit of money. It'll make room in the bank for the next lot that comes in.' It was a novel idea. It made Pel feel good to know that at least his home life was a roaring success, although he wasn't sure how.

16

De Troq' left early to make his enquiries in Montauban, leaving Darcy to see the two old peasants known as Radio Itzac. Although their ramshackle house wasn't far away, Kate suggested taking him in her old car, saying that they didn't take kindly to strangers, especially policemen, and that perhaps it would be better if she accompanied him.

Jo-jo, the Perrier bottle, was there to keep an eye on the children, so as the sunshine revved up to scorching, they clattered down the driveway in the Quatre L, her ancient Renault 4, to see the two old boys.

The house sat in the middle of a vineyard, looking as if it had been dropped there, violently, by a passing plane. The roof was in disarray, the walls were crumbling and most of the shutters were hanging from only one hinge. The door was wide open and inside they could see a grubby kitchen where a balding chicken was happily roosting on the fridge. Kate knocked at the window and stood back to wait. Suddenly, a gaggle of geese flew down the wooden staircase opposite, leaving their calling cards on every step. They disappeared with a flurry of wings and shouting loudly into the vineyard, to be followed by a dirty little wrinkled old man brandishing a stick at them and slipping wildly in what they had deposited on the stairs.

'Bloody geese,' he shouted. 'Came and woke me up. Upstairs in my bedroom! Blasé must've forgot to close the door last night. Silly old *con*.'

Putting his stick down by the door he offered his hand to greet Darcy, then lifted his unshaven face to Kate for the customary peck on both cheeks. '*Attention*,' he said gaily. '*Ca pique!*'

They were ushered inside to the kitchen where the ageing chicken sat cosily in the corner. As the old boy went to the fridge to find some milk he lifted a hand to lovingly stroke the bird's scraggy neck.

Darcy raised his eyebrows and looked questioningly at Kate.

'She broke a leg,' she explained calmly, as if it was all perfectly normal. 'Monsieur Raffi splinted it and put her to recuperate on the fridge. She's been there ever since.'

'Lays an occasional egg too,' Raffi added proudly, smiling a toothless smile at them. Darcy had, in his amusement, been smiling too, but when he saw the old man's broken teeth he snapped his mouth closed. My teeth may be broken, he thought, but at least those that are left are white. Raffi's were blackened stumps, as if they'd been caught in a forest fire.

While Raffi was pottering about, heating his milk on the single gas ring, they were joined by another equally old and wrinkled man. He was tall, a good deal thinner, but just as sordid-looking as Raffi.

Kate introduced him as Monsieur Blasé and they went through the hand-shaking and cheek-kissing routine one more time. Even the two old boys shook hands as it was the first time that morning they'd seen each other.

'Bah!' Blasé exclaimed seeing the warm milk in Raffi's other hand. 'Don't know how you can drink that muck. Must go back to when he was at his mother's breast. Bah!' He opened a cupboard by removing the door – the hinges had long since ceased to function – and found himself a half-full bottle of wine.

While the two old men breakfasted, one on bread and milk, the other on *saucisson* and wine, Kate explained why they'd come to see them.

Surprisingly, they seemed delighted and only too willing to tell them all they knew about the house across the river,

'Owner's name is Incks,' Raffi said.

'Englishman,' Blasé added.

'Never seen him, mind.'

'Never there.'

'Had part of it done up, he has, probably for his holidays.'

'Or to hide.'

They were like a Laurel and Hardy sketch and Kate was having difficulty smothering a smile. Darcy, however, hardened by long years of police work, took them very seriously.

'Hide what?' he asked.

'Don't know.'

'Like a fortress, that place.'

'Been round and round but we couldn't get in.'

'And if *we* couldn't get in . . .' Blasé left the sentence unfinished to take a gulp from his bottle of wine.

Raffi was dunking his stale bread into the warm milk. 'He thinks he's a spy,' he offered, indicating his companion with a dripping lump of bread.

'Why?'

'Don't know, just a feeling.'

'He worked in the Resistance during the war. Still thinks it's going on.'

'I *ran* the Resistance here,' Blasé corrected importantly. 'And as for the war, it certainly isn't over yet. Everyone's still fighting everyone, they just call it a different name now. It's peaceful enough out here in the countryside, but look at our cities, French versus Arab, student versus teacher, farmers versus everyone, and it won't get any better. I've seen how they organise their strikes nowadays, can be violent. Then there's the football hooligans. This is supposed to be peacetime.' He snorted. 'There are atrocities happening right now, here in France. Kids

124

being beaten to a pulp by their parents, men demoralised by years on the dole, women raped by sex maniacs. Peace! For how long?'

'He's been wondering that ever since 1945.'

When they left, Blasé remained at the table to finish his bottle of wine, but Raffi came into the yard with them. 'Shouldn't listen too much to him if I was you,' he whispered loudly. 'He's always exaggerating. Never sober, you see.'

Even so, Darcy didn't think the old man was such a fool; anyone capable of running the Resistance during the Second World War would have had his wits about him. On the other hand, that was a long time ago, and he had consumed nearly half a litre of wine on an almost empty stomach. If he did that every day he could easily have pickled his brain since the war.

At midday de Troq' phoned the château. He was stuck in the files at Sécurité Sociale and expected to be there for the rest of the afternoon. Taking advantage of the baron's prolonged absence, Darcy invited Kate to join him for lunch away from home, the kids, the bottle of Perrier and the monster dog, Rasputin, who still had a tendency to look hungry every time he clapped eyes on Darcy. After only a moment's hesitation Kate accepted, suggesting that they should go in the other car.

'What other car?'

'The one thing, apart from my sons, that was worth salvaging from my marriage.' She laughed and crossed the yard to two large barn doors. Sitting inside, slightly dusty but magnificent all the same, was a blue Bentley.

She climbed in and brought the car out of hiding, leaving it purring quietly in the sunshine, like a contented tiger, as she folded the top down.

'A convertible too,' she said. 'It was my wedding present from my ex-husband. But I never drove the thing up there on the Scottish border, it was always blowing an arctic gale.'

'And here?'

'I don't get it out often, it makes the locals' eyes boggle. But once in a while it's fun. Do you want to drive?'

De Troq' certainly would have, so Darcy climbed in behind the wheel.

Kate was full of surprises and he hoped she wasn't mixed up in something she shouldn't be. It had occurred to him that she was very involved one way or another in a number of curious events, and there were a lot of questions that still remained unanswered. He knew her background from what Madame Pel had told him, but her sudden disappearance from her politician husband and England made him wonder. What had she been doing in the mean time? What did she live on – she had to have money? Why had Georges Durand come to her for help instead of to his brother? Was it simply that she had the keys to a perfect hideout or something else? But why had she contacted Pel? Could it be the classic criminal coup, a diversion? Darcy didn't want to think so, but it was a possibility he couldn't ignore.

17

They seemed to be getting nowhere fast. Pel pushed his
spectacles up on to the top of his head. The files in front
of him showed a definite connection between the two
murders and the Margay robbery, but while his officers
continued to make their enquiries and type out their
reports, they were no further on than before. The Chief
had asked for a bit more action and Pel had promised it,
but in which direction? It was turning out to be a terrible
waiting game. They still hadn't worked out the puzzle over
the alarm. The *maire* had come personally into the Hôtel de
Police to inform them that Margay had in fact applied for
planning permission for his factory outside the city, and
he was hoping for an early conclusion to the break-in.
He told the Chief, confidentially, that Margay had been
making noises about perhaps going elsewhere, so could
the police please get a move on. The Chief passed on the
information to Pel, confidentially of course. Pel would
have liked the American to move to another area, but a
break-in was a break-in even though it was a cowboy's
house and Pel didn't like the man. As he'd pointed out to
the Chief, he was, after all, entitled to the same treatment
as any other owner of a property that had been robbed.

He'd had no word from Goschen in London, Cousin
Roger had nothing to offer, and de Troq' and Darcy
were a long way away producing a lot of questions
but very few answers. So far all they had given him,

apart from a headache, was the identity of the Shrew and the suggestion by a couple of drunks that Incks was a spy. Brisard, the *juge d'instruction*, had started leaning on him too.

'Results,' he said, standing in front of Pel like a fat schoolmaster, brandishing his cane and full of self-importance. 'That's what we need, and so far we have very little. It isn't good for the city to have two murders still unsolved on its conscience, and the robbery of such an important and charming man as Margay is none too good either. I shall have to make my own enquiries and see if I can find something you've overlooked.'

Pompous, repetitive ass, thought Pel. 'That is your privilege,' he said, however, through clenched teeth, hoping he wasn't going to have to endure his presence much longer. 'I wish you luck,' he added when finally Brisard's wide hips negotiated the doorway to leave.

When Pel reached home that evening his wife hadn't yet arrived. Madame Routy was slamming saucepans around in the kitchen and came out briefly to reassure herself that it was indeed her employer who had entered the house and not a rapist. Although, by the look on her face when she saw Pel, he felt that perhaps she would have preferred a rapist. However, she poured him a small whisky, about a thimbleful – she knew exactly where the bottle was kept, Pel noticed, even though he'd hidden it carefully behind all the other bottles – and handed him his drink as if she hoped he'd choke on it.

The slamming of saucepans resumed with the normal ferocity, making Pel feel it might be wiser to leave her to it and take a stroll in the garden.

Yves Pasquier was by the hole in the hedge with his shaggy mongrel. Once again Pel greeted the wrong end.

'How was *Star Wars*?' Pel asked seriously. Seeing the scratches and bruises up and down Yves' legs, he wondered if the boy had taken part in it himself.

'*Génial*! The robots were really great. You know, they

actually had to make huge remote-controlled models for the film, it's amazing how they did it. They can do anything with electronics these days. I think I might do that when I grow up.'

'I thought you wanted to be a policeman?' Pel asked indignantly. He approved of small boys wanting to be policemen.

'Oh, I do, but I thought I could be one of your experts. You know, who invents an electronic thing that could catch criminals, that sort of thing. After all, you have computers already, don't you?'

Pel was horrified. A remote-controlled thing to catch criminals – he'd be out of a job! Debray had at last returned from Paris after his advanced course in computers and was blinding everyone with science, showing them what they could do with the machines they had at the Hôtel de Police. Pel hadn't understood a word. He hadn't wanted to.

While Pel sat down to a quiet supper with his wife, Darcy and de Troq' were sitting down to a very noisy one with Kate. Pierre and his Perrier bottle wife with their two children had joined them for the meal again and it was turning out to be a riotous event. Pierre and the four children had been setting something up for their entertainment and when the meal was finished Pierre went off to put it into action. As he came back from the other side of the yard he was fiddling with a small black box in his hands.

There was a sudden explosion by the duck pond followed by what sounded like rapid gunfire. Both Darcy and de Troq' leapt to their feet ready to defend the château, believing they were under attack. But Pierre roared with laughter.

'They're only *pétards*, bangers,' he said. 'The boys love them. They're on sale in a lot of toy shops. Personally I think they're too damn dangerous for kids. Look at this one.' He held out his hand and offered Darcy what looked like a large stick of dynamite covered in red paper.

'Kids can buy these things in toy shops?'

'Yes, and listen to the bang it makes.' The boys were bouncing up and down at Pierre's side.

Pierre lit the end of the protruding blue string and threw the large firework across the yard. It fizzed for a moment then exploded with such a noise it could easily have been mistaken for a small bomb.

'Imagine if it went off in the wrong place,' Pierre said seriously, 'like in one of the boys' pockets.'

Darcy and de Troq' looked at each other. 'So what are you doing larking about with them?' Darcy asked.

'Boys will be boys,' Pierre replied. 'I'd rather demonstrate them than have the kids handle them themselves. With a bit of cunning I can lengthen the fuse and plant them all round the yard, coming back to set them off by remote control. It minimises the danger. Easy when you know how.'

'Do you often give little demonstrations like this?'

'No, but with the fourteenth of July coming up, I've been asked to set up a display of fireworks, not bangers, for the village. I wanted to test the lighting sequence. I don't want any mishaps with all those people around.'

Pierre, they thought, had hidden talents. He deserved a little more attention.

When the evening's excitement had subsided de Troq' asked him what he did for a living.

'I'm an electrician. But not *just* an electrician,' he said proudly. 'I install remote-control shutters and sunshades, cookers and alarms. You'd be surprised what can be done by remote control. I work a lot for the handicapped. To them, remote control is not an expensive luxury, it simply makes their difficult lives a bit easier.'

They had another question for him.

'An alarm system, a very sophisticated alarm system, connected to a house's electricity supply, plus batteries to back it up in case of an electricity cut.' Pierre looked interested and leant forward to concentrate. 'The alarm system works perfectly on, say, Friday night. It also works perfectly on, say, Monday morning. It hasn't been tampered with, no polystyrene sprayed from an aerosol to deaden the noise, no wires cut, no fingerprints. The alarm is exactly as it was on Friday night. However, on Monday morning it's discovered that the house has been well and truly robbed. No one heard the alarm, and believe me, if it had gone off, someone would have heard it. How did they do it?'

'Easy,' Pierre said delightedly.

'Go on.' The policemen were all ears.

'Where's your electricity meter, Kate?'

'Out in one of the barns.'

'Mine's outside the back door. Electricity meters are placed outside so that when they come to read them they don't have to disturb the occupants, or wait for them to be in. The bloke just turns up, reads the meter and buggers off. No one has to wait in and miss precious hours of work. A very sensible and convenient system. To cut the electricity it's just as easy. If a house owner hasn't paid his bill, the bloke from the EDF, Electricité de France, rolls up in his little blue Renault van, switches off the current with a flick of a switch, locks and seals the meter box and off he goes. No knocking on doors, no arguments. Trouble is, it's just as easy for a burglar. He flicks the switch and the alarm is no longer operational because there's no electricity.'

'But there was a large battery, as a safeguard, and that was in the house,' de Troq' pointed out. 'That works automatically if there's no power from outside.'

'No problem. When the electricity supply is cut off, the battery takes over, agreed. It supplies the current for all those wonderful little electronic beams so necessary to an effective alarm system. But the battery is there to cover a temporary cut, of perhaps a few minutes even a few hours. It wouldn't last longer than twenty-four hours at the most. After that the battery would be completely flat. No electricity, no battery, no alarm. Switch off the electrics on Saturday night, the battery would be flat by Sunday night – you could walk into a house that was completely unprotected.'

'But it was working again on Monday morning.'

'Of course. The burglar, having finished burgling, steps round to the meter again, having made sure that he's carefully closed all the doors and windows and not left one of his mates inside, flicks the switch, and on goes the electricity. The alarm is active again. According to its beady little electronic eyes, nothing is moving, there's no body heat present, so all is well. It doesn't ring.'

'Remarkably easy really,' Darcy commented.

'If you know how.'

'Who else would know how?'

'Any decent electrician with a bit of brain and the desire to work it out. My brother, for instance, Georges – he'd know. He's an expert in air-conditioning, but an electrician all the same.' Pierre's voice had lost its excitement when he spoke of his brother. He was taking his disappearance badly and had more than once taken Darcy or de Troq' to one side to beg them to find him. However, at that moment what he had said sent de Troq's mind buzzing back to Margay Manor.

'Air-conditioning?' he asked slowly.

'Yes, I taught him about electricity, but he decided there was more money to be made in installing air-conditioning in foreigners' houses. In fact he's just finished a big job up your way for an American. He said he was very well paid.'

Light was dawning on the Margay case. De Troq' asked Pierre the name of the American, but he was unable to tell him, only that Georges was very pleased to have got the contract.

'Does your brother work with anyone else?' de Troq'

asked, not wanting to let the subject drop. 'Someone by the name of Bargiacchi, for instance?' It was a long shot but worth a try and by the look on Pierre's face he'd struck gold.

'My brother *is* the chap called Bargiacchi,' he said quietly.

I thought your name was Durand?' Kate interjected with surprise.

'Mine is, but my brother's name is Bargiacchi. When my mother came to France from Italy after the war, she married a Frenchman called Durand, my father. When I was eight he ran off with another woman. She had a couple of difficult years but eventually she took up with an Italian she'd met. I think she'd lost confidence in Frenchmen, and the Italian, Bargiacchi, came to live with us. She eventually had another son, Giorgio, my half-brother. Bargiacchi was always in trouble though and was finally sent to prison for half murdering a friend of his.'

'It was his partner in crime, he shopped him,' de Troq' pointed out.

'How do you know?'

'It's on record.'

'Well, that may be the case. While he was in prison my mother died of cancer and we never saw Bargiacchi again. Even when he came out he never came near us, so I had to take care of Giorgio as best I could until he came of age.'

'I think I should tell you that we are looking for your brother with regard to the robbery of a Monsieur Margay, just outside Dijon.' There seemed little point at this stage in telling Pierre about the two murders they believed were connected to the robbery. It might just frighten him off, and so far he'd been more than helpful.

Pierre was frowning as he took his wife's hand. 'I think young Georges has got a bit of explaining to do,' he said to no one in particular. 'I tried to keep him on the straight and narrow, and I thought I'd succeeded, but it looks as if the Bargiacchi habit has been inherited.'

Considering their family history, Pierre had been remarkably deceived. De Troq' wasn't completely convinced and wondered if Georges was in fact capable of murder. He said nothing, however, asking instead about the other brother in the family, Giuseppe.

'That's me,' Pierre said. 'When my mother died I changed my name to Pierre. I lived and worked in France, and had every intention of staying. I'd never liked my given name, it got me teased at school, and made my girlfriends laugh.'

Pel would have understood, Darcy thought, laden down as he was with a string of hefty names, Clovis, Evariste, Désiré, it was enough to make a man worry rats. Mothers should be more careful when choosing their offspring's names.

'I didn't laugh,' Jo-jo said to her husband.

'That's why I married you.'

18

It had turned out to be a surprising evening. De Troq' rang Pel at home to tell him what they had discovered. He'd been sleeping peacefully and was not best pleased at being disturbed, but he was cheered up by their news. However, after what he'd heard he couldn't close his eyes again and arrived at the Hôtel de Police the following morning feeling suitably persecuted, in a thoroughly foul mood, and already lighting his second cigarette. The foul mood increased when he noticed Misset back at work.

'What are you doing here on a Sunday?' he bellowed.

'Thought I'd look in and see if you were all still alive.'

'Well, I'm half dead, so don't get in my way.' Pel pushed past and slammed his office door daring anyone, especially Misset, to interrupt his thoughts.

Normally he wouldn't have been there himself on a Sunday, but things at last seemed to be moving, so before preparing for lunch at Cousin Roger's he'd slipped away briefly to check through the details once more and to see if Goschen had at last called from London. He hadn't, and Pel sat for a good hour staring at his files looking for something that apparently wasn't there. He was sure that although the robbery and the murders were connected there was something more. Something much more important that was worth killing for. He knew very well that murders were committed for trifling reasons, sometimes in panic, sometimes through greed, sometimes fear. But this one smelt different, it smelt well organised. There was a plan behind it, but what the hell was it? Where did they go now?

He'd found no answers by the time he returned to his anxious wife who was quietly sitting ready and waiting to leave for Cousin Roger's. They were late arriving, but it made no difference. It was still chaos, with children and animals under everyone's feet, and the noise level in danger of reaching burglar alarm level. The meal, however, was copious and well worth suffering the inconvenience of the numerous offspring. Afterwards, while the two wives were tidying up in the kitchen, Cousin Roger suggested a look at his new rose bush. Pel knew very well that he was about as keen a gardener as Pel himself was and recognised this as an excuse to disappear for a quick drag. He followed him happily out into the garden. As they stepped through the french windows of the *salon*, Cousin Roger tipped the dregs of his cognac into the fish tank.

'It must be a boring life swimming round and round in circles. I think they like you coming over, they always get a tot to jigger them up.'

'So,' Pel said as they installed themselves round a limp-looking rose bush. They both had cigarettes in their hands and were luxuriously drawing the smoke down to their socks. 'What have you found out about our famous friend Margay?'

'Not a lot, I'm afraid. He seems to be exactly what he says he is. He arrived from New York to make a tour of Europe – you know the sort of thing, London, Paris and Rome in ten days – along with an ordinary group of tourists, but he didn't leave with them. He stayed, sent for his colleagues from across the Atlantic and set up house. He's been back and forth a couple of times looking for likely places to open a factory.'

'Looks like he found what he was looking for.'

'The application has gone in to start building just outside the city limits on the *zone industrielle*. He is well thought

136

of and obviously has a lot of money. I think he'll get his permission.'

'What's the factory for?' Pel asked casually, pretending to study the one and only faded bloom on the rose bush in front of him, but in fact enjoying the glorious odour of his newly lit Gauloise.

'Computerised toys, hand-held electronic games, that sort of thing. He's going to import the components from Hong Kong and assemble the bits here.'

Pel was no longer studying the rose bush, he was studying Cousin Roger.

'Hong Kong?'

'That's what I've heard. Crateloads of gadgets to be assembled here in France. The idea is that he can then label them "Made in France" which pleases any number of chaps concerned with improving our trade figures. It's also a good selling point, I suppose.'

Darcy wasn't enjoying his Sunday. He'd come down on to the terrace in the yard to breakfast with the rest of the family in the already hot sunshine, to hear Kate proposing taking the horses out for a gallop. De Troq' was at the table and enthusing wildly. Trust him to know how to ride, Darcy thought bitterly. He'd never set foot on a horse, and wasn't sure he wanted to. So while he sat alone, watching the children make mud pies in the dust with a bucket of water, Kate and de Troq' disappeared over the horizon with the two horses.

Kate had looked seductive seated on her huge black horse – come to that, he had to admit de Troq' had looked pretty good too. They were made for each other. He was startled to find he was feeling madly jealous, something he wasn't used to. In the past he had always been the one to disappear into the sunset with a beautiful woman; he'd never had any difficulty in recognising the green lights in a girl's eyes, or getting them into bed for a quick display of gymnastics. But Kate was different. She wasn't just a pretty face, there was something else too – but there'd been no green lights in his direction. He hadn't noticed any in de Troq's either. Perhaps he was losing his touch. Sadly he thought about his lost girlfriend. Silly bitch, fancy leaving him for a set of teeth, half a set of teeth even. In fact, now he thought about it calmly, she'd been just a bit too quick off the mark with her departure. Almost as if she'd been waiting for the excuse. She obviously hadn't loved him very much to go so fast. Perhaps there'd been someone else? He was surprised to find that although his pride was still hurt, as any man would expect after losing his girl, it hurt less with each day and he came to the conclusion that perhaps he hadn't loved her as much as he had thought either. Perhaps he ought to learn to ride.

He suggested it when Kate and de Troq' finally returned.

'Of course,' Kate replied happily. 'Now would be a good time. After the gallop they've just had they'll be much quieter. Get up on to Jess and I'll take you down the lane on the leading rein.'

Quelle honte!

Darcy allowed himself to be led out of the yard and began to think it was all pretty easy. Until Kate suggested a trot. It was worse than Pel's old car, it shook every bone in his body.

He didn't know it but it was the start of something big.

19

All hell had broken loose! Pel snatched up the phone and dialled the Tarn number de Troq' had given him. He had to wait while de Troq' was fetched from the barn but when he heard his voice Pel's instructions were loud and clear.

'Get back here at once,' he shouted. 'Margay's been kidnapped and I need you. Tell Darcy I've had another letter from Professor Henri. I'm faxing it to Albi today. Tell him to get over there and get on with it.'

Pierre appeared in the yard as de Troq' was preparing his car to leave. He handed him a sheet of paper.

'It doesn't mean anything to me,' he explained, 'but it might mean something to your experts. I found it at the cottage where Georges has been hiding.'

Madame Barrau, the Guardian's wife, was their only witness. She was sitting importantly in front of Pel's desk telling him and the Chief all about it. Downstairs the newspapermen were clamouring at the doors. The story of the robbery was old news, even the murders stirred little interest now, and the newspapermen were after something fresh. Margay's kidnapping was just the thing. However, the police had refused to make a statement for the time being and they were becoming impatient.

De Troq' pushed his way through the crowd and made his way upstairs to Pel's office. It was late in the afternoon and he was tired from the drive north, but he had a feeling there'd be little rest from now on.

During the morning Pel had been out to Margay Manor with the usual crowd – Fingerprints, Forensics, Photography – and had come away knowing only that Margay had been taken from the front of his house and that Madame Barrau had seen it. At least someone for once had seen something.

'There was shooting,' she said, 'lots of shooting. That's what attracted my attention. I was coming down the hill towards the house to do my usual chores – you know, washing up and that, and to prepare Monsieur Margay's lunch. He loves my French cooking –'

'And?' Pel had no intention of letting her divert into rhapsodies over her culinary expertise.

'And I heard banging. I thought at first it was my Bécane, the old moped I ride. I thought it was backfiring or something, so I stopped to take a look at it or even a quick kick at it, blasted thing. It bucked me off once, and I can still feel it in my back. I wasn't going to have that happen again. But when I stopped the motor, I heard the noise again. It was shooting! Funny, I thought, the hunting season isn't for months, then I realised it was coming from Monsieur Margay's house. It was quite some distance away still, but I've got good eyesight and I knew it was Monsieur the moment I looked. He was brought round the side of the car and bundled in.'

'Can you tell us anything about the car?'

'It was black, it was big, a bit like Monsieur's Mercedes but it wasn't the same, it wasn't quite as big. But it was big all the same.'

'Thank you, madame,' the Chief interjected before she got herself too tangled up in details. 'Please go on.'

'Well, there was a lot of shouting. I couldn't hear what they were shouting, just raised voices, angry, you know. Then the car doors slammed and off they went.'

'How many men were there, apart from Margay?'

'Three, I think, yes, three, all dressed alike too.'

'You saw what they were wearing?' It seemed unlikely, but Madame's eyesight was good after many years' experience as a nosy-parker.

'Well, not exactly. But I can tell you they were all wearing hats.'

'Cowboy hats?' Pel suggested.

The look Madame Barrau shot across the desk let him know she thought the idea utterly ridiculous. 'No,' she sniffed, 'ordinary hats.'

'Three men, all wearing hats, ordinary hats, bundled Margay into a large, but not very large, black car,' Pel reiterated for her. 'Then what happened?'

'They drove down the drive towards me. They sent the gravel flying as they turned into the lane – nearly sent me flying, for that matter. I had to jump out of the way.'

'And your moped?'

'I landed on top of it. That's why I was at the hospital all morning, having my poor leg bandaged. I don't know how I shall work now.'

'With Monsieur Margay not there you'll be able to rest, perhaps?'

Madame Barrau gave Pel another withering look. 'That's not all I do, you know,' she snorted. 'There's still the house and the poultry, and my husband's family's coming over again soon.'

When Madame Barrau had left, Pel went down to see the press to give them the bare essentials and nothing else. The Chief was under pressure from all sides and was requesting discretion. But the newspapermen weren't satisfied as Pel came to the end of his statement. Pel, however, wasn't saying any more; he knew they'd probably make up the rest anyway.

As he made his way back up to his office he collided with a red-haired thunderbolt.

'Annie Saxe! Calm down. I know it's panic stations here but I won't have my staff cantering in the corridors.'

141

'Sorry, sir, but it's important. Your man in London, he's on the phone.'

Back in his office, Pel reached for the phone. 'Charles L. Incks', Goschen told him, 'is a civil servant, a junior attaché in the Ministry of Agriculture, Fisheries and Food. He's been a bit difficult to find out about. I gather he's well protected on all sides from any prying questions. Until recently he was unimportant, simply occupying a desk at the ministry and running errands. However, during the last eighteen months it has come to someone's attention that he's a computer genius. How or why I can't find out – when I mentioned his name mouths shut like steel traps – but sufficient to say, when this discovery was made he rapidly found himself at a desk the size of his previous office and getting everyone else running the errands. He's flown round the world a couple of times since then, taking part in international conferences as the expert behind Britain's official representative. His rise to fame has been fast and furious. It has been proposed, unexpectedly, but justifiably, that he should be our man in Toulouse to oversee the European weather satellite.'

So that's where Pel had heard the name before. Yves Pasquier, his young next-door neighbour, had told him of the satellite and of the Englishman coming to France.

It set Pel thinking. He reached for the packet of Gauloises. Just one, he told himself, to help his brain tick. There had been a lot of talk about computers recently. Margay was trying to get permission to build a factory to put together components from Hong Kong to make computer games. Incks was an electronics and computer genius and owned a house near Montauban, which is where Margay had been when his own house was robbed. Could it be that Georges Bargiacchi broke into Margay Manor and found something more interesting than he expected? Could he have stumbled on plans for the illegal copying and trafficking of computer games and videos? Was it in fact Margay's men who had committed

142

murder in an attempt to retrieve the incriminating papers? It seemed to Pel highly likely. People had murdered for a great deal less, and computer games and videos were big money nowadays. The illegal copying for resale carried heavy penalties.

Something else occurred to him as he finished the last soothing drags of his cigarette. Vlaxi had had a computer on his desk too, and he had claimed to play the stock market. Could he also be involved, but at a different level? It all seemed very possible. The three crimes, the two murders and the robbery of the American, were connected, he knew that now. There had been too many coincidences for it to be otherwise. Computers seemed to be the missing link. Had that been what Professor Henri had meant? Was he trying to tell Pel that Charles L. Incks was the brains behind it all who made Vlaxi and Margay play the game? He took out the second letter he'd received from Hong Kong and stared at it.

'Finding the Chinese language difficult, these chaps talk in pictures. Been told the Catmen are seeing stars. Hope it means something to you.'

Pel thought that at last the Professor's messages were indeed beginning to make sense. If they were copying videos of famous films too, that would be the stars they were seeing – film stars! But the 'Catmen' still had him foxed. Kate had suggested that L. Incks could be misheard as lynx, but Catmen was plural, so who were the others? Or could it simply be a code name for the men who were working with L. Incks?

He sat back, reasonably satisfied. At last they were getting somewhere. It was all supposition, but the only thing they had to do now was find the proof. Or Georges Bargiacchi. That was would be more difficult.

Although Pel was feeling satisfied, there was still something that baffled him. Why had Margay been kidnapped? Was he double-crossing someone? Vlaxi, for instance? Or was the whole affair more complicated than that? It was almost too simple.

He stubbed out his cigarette viciously and picked up the phone. It was only a matter of seconds before he was speaking to Darcy and telling him to find out more about Incks.

'If he owns a house down there,' he said, 'he must have dealt with the local *notaire* for the legalities of a house purchase, plus possibly an estate agent. If repairs have been made to the house someone must have been paid to do them. See if you can find out what this man looks like, at least. Goschen knows about him but there are no photographs available. The English seem to be treating him as some sort of highly secret weapon. I want to know why, and fast. And', he added, 'see if there's anything going on at his house. Margay's disappeared and I have a feeling he may just turn up down there.'

As he put the phone down there was a knock on the door. Leguyader came in.

Pel was in no mood to listen to the walking Encyclopedia Larousse, which was what the man from Forensics so often sounded like, but he had to be patient enough to find out if there was anything interesting at Margay Manor. Spent bullets from a rare pistol, scratched messages in the newly laid gravel – Pel was only hoping for miracles.

'Inform me,' he said, lighting another cigarette without noticing what he was doing.

'You'll kill yourself smoking like that,' Leguyader said cheerfully. 'Did you know that thousands of French citizens die of smoking every year? It's responsible for 90 per cent of all cancers. It increases the risk of heart disease by a factor of two to three. Then there's bronchitis –'

Pel didn't want to know. 'Yes, I'm sure you're right, but in the mean time duty calls. Let's have your report.'

'It was only a suggestion. You really ought to try and cut down.'

'If I cut down on cigarettes, will you cut down on useless information?' Check mate!

'The information I have to offer you', Leguyader went on pompously, 'is anything but useless. You may find it very interesting. That is, if you have the time between puffing on your death sticks to listen.'

'Very well,' Pel replied as he resentfully extinguished his cigarette. 'Peace is declared.' But not for long, he thought. 'Now please, *accouche*, get on with it.' Pel was hanging on to his patience by the skin of his teeth.

'I went up to the manor to examine the shot marks, expecting to find a number of them in the exterior stonework of the house, or at least one spent cartridge in the gravel or flowerbeds round the house. In fact I found nothing.'

'Nothing! Madame Barrau said she heard shooting, lots of it.'

'Exactly, but I found no evidence of it.'

'Are you suggesting that she made it all up?'

'Or that they were shooting blanks. They make the same noise but don't do any damage. And another thing, the gravel on the driveway is deep, it hasn't been there long, it's thick and evenly laid. There was no sign of a scuffle. No dragged footprints, no deep indentations to indicate someone moving at speed, perhaps in panic. All I found were the usual gentle undulations made by normal, relatively slow-moving feet.'

'So Margay went quietly.'

'And he locked the front door before he left.' Leguyader was enjoying himself. Sometimes telling Pel he'd found nothing was more satisfying than coming up with the information he'd been waiting for.

'No blood?' Pel thought he might just as well ask.

'Not a drop.'

'Then it was a very gentle kidnapping, with only one witness, perfectly positioned to see it all. Curiouser and curiouser.'

145

20

Darcy had nothing either. He'd spent all morning on the phone trying to find out something more about Incks, but no one had seen him. He had been told the house and repairs had been negotiated by a firm operating in Marzac, which turned out to be an Englishman with an untidy desk in his living-room. From there he represented a company of estate agents in London and had never clapped eyes on Incks. He had sent information to London and had received instructions back. Money had always been received by cheque from the London office and it was the English agent from Marzac who had signed the *L'acte sous-seing privé* and the *acte finale* purchasing the house in the name of Incks. It was a practice fairly often carried out for the benefit of foreign buyers who couldn't actually be present for all the various formalities. The address given on the Act of Sale was Incks, Whitehall, London, which as Kate explained was as anonymous as saying Montmartre, Paris. Whitehall covered a very large area, filled with office blocks and government departments. With Kate's help they finally managed to contact the London office responsible for dealing with the sale of the house and the exchange of moneys, but they too told them all instructions were received by post, from the same address.

'What about the cheque?' Darcy urged. 'Ask them what address was on the cheque.'

But Kate had put the phone down. 'There's no point, Daniel. English cheques don't carry your home address as they do in France.'

'Well, who did they write to when they needed to? They must have at some point in the negotiations.'

'It seems Incks, or someone calling himself Incks, phoned them for information. Any papers that needed signing were picked up by a private courier. They don't remember which one, there are thousands in London.'

'So we've come to another dead end.'

'Not entirely,' Kate said. 'Pel wants Incks' house watched. I think we'd better get over there.'

Before Darcy could protest, she continued, 'I'm coming with you, Daniel. It's a lonely place and there's no telephone. What would you do if you needed help? If I'm there at least I'll be able to get back across the forest and contact someone. Besides,' she added, clinching the deal, 'you don't know your way throught the forest. It's as big as Paris and easier to get lost in there than in a city – there are no street names, no historic monuments, no river in the middle, no taxis, no one to ask, just trees. Large stout oak trees. Many a time search parties have been sent in, and often they've arrived too late. It's a wild place, you know!' She was exaggerating but it worked. 'You need me as a guide.'

'On horseback!' Darcy sounded as if he'd been invited to pilot a one-way rocket to Mars.

'It's the only way,' Kate explained. 'To get there by car we'd have to go virtually all the way to Montauban and take the forest track back from the other side. Even then it's a long way through the trees. It's quicker on horseback, even if we don't gallop.'

Gallop! God forbid! It was all Darcy could do to stay in the saddle at a slow trot.

Kate saddled up the two horses and helped Darcy up

on to Jess, then she swung herself gracefully on to Bebel's back. He whinnied and reared up in excitement; the pair of them looked like something off a cowboy film set, or Zorro's equal. Darcy sat slumped in the saddle admiring them until it occurred to him that Jess, beneath him, might be getting ideas. As he straightened up and clung for dear life, they set off gently in the hot afternoon sun, walking slowly down the road towards the immense forest behind the house. As they entered the shade of the dense oak trees Darcy began to feel more at ease. So far he'd managed not to disgrace himself, and anyway he was attached to Kate by the leading rein. The sun winked through the overhead foliage, making bright yellow moving spots on the ground beneath them. There was a deafening silence that hung heavily among the thick branches. No longer could they hear the distant chug of an ancient tractor; there were no cars, no voices, nothing. Darcy sat back comfortably to enjoy the peace and quiet. Not for long.

'Feel like a canter, Daniel?'

Kate urged Bebel forward and the horse bounced happily into a canter, hauling the unwilling Darcy along behind like a speedboat dragging a tender. In fact he found cantering easier than trotting, but hung on the pommel of the saddle all the same as if his life depended on it – he suspected it might. Suddenly anxious, he hoped the girth was tight enough to keep both him and the saddle where they were supposed to be.

Darcy felt he was getting the hang of this riding business. It wasn't so difficult after all, he thought, but when the horses slowed back to a trot he decided he'd made a mistake as his remaining teeth rattled in their sockets. Mercifully, they slowed to a walk almost immediately and he was able to draw breath and relax again.

'You were born to it,' Kate said, smiling back at him. 'How do you feel?'

'Better in overdrive than in second gear,' he grinned.

'I've been thinking,' he went on, 'while I wasn't terrified of falling off. Did you know about Pierre's brother and the family history?' It had bothered him that she may have known more than she was letting on. He would have liked to be sure she was innocent and not mixed up in what looked like developing into a very sordid affair.

'I knew they were brothers, of course,' she replied, 'well, half-brothers, but Georges I've only seen a couple of times. I never asked him what his surname was, I suppose I simply assumed it was the same as Pierre's, Durand. I also knew his mother was Italian and that his father had run off with another woman, but you know, I don't encourage questions about my past, I feel it's better left where it is, firmly in the past. I made a mistake marrying too young to the wrong man. So I suppose I don't pry into other people's lives.'

He accepted her explanation without comment, still wondering whether it was the whole truth. It could be, he conceded; she'd never once asked about his own private life. Perhaps she wasn't interested.

For the rest of the ride he let her lead in silence, relaxing when they walked, hanging on when they cantered and wishing horses had brake-pedals when they trotted. However, he managed to stay upright and finally they reached the riverside. As they slid from the saddle to lead the horses down a precarious slope they could see the tiny cottage nestling in a small sunlit clearing at the edge of the water.

It was early evening by the time they'd tethered the horses out of sight behind the house and settled down to wait. It was going to be a long night. Not that Darcy minded spending it in a lonely fisherman's cottage with a pretty woman: he simply wished they knew more about each other. Their lack of conversation was making him feel uncomfortable.

' 'I know you don't like prying into other people's lives,' he ventured, 'but it looks as if we've got quite a wait ahead

149

of us. Wouldn't you like to know a bit about the man you're going to spend the night with?'

She laughed as she unfastened the pony-tail in the nape of her neck, shaking out her long hair and passing a hand casually through the tresses that had fallen across her forehead. 'If you want to tell me,' she sighed, 'but I'll ask you no questions, just say what you feel like saying.'

'For instance,' he suggested, 'wouldn't you like to know why I've only got half a set of teeth?'

'Daniel,' she replied softly, looking at him from beneath her thick lashes, 'I think there's a great deal more to you than a set of teeth. It's not a set of snappers that makes a man.'

Music to his ears. He told her anyway and finished up unexpectedly telling her about the departure of his girlfriend.

'I think she cared more about the way you look than the way you are,' she said simply.

She was right and he knew it. They fell silent for a moment until Kate got up from the window, where she'd been listening to the story of Darcy's life, and suggested something to drink. 'It's nearly seven o'clock, after all,' she said. 'We'll have a *coup de rouge*, then if you like I'll give you the abridged version of my leaving England.'

They sat together talking quietly, Kate explaining her disillusionment at her marriage, Darcy listening sympathetically, pleased to know more about her, understanding at last that she had nothing to hide. He got the impression that it was the first time that she'd really explained it to anyone.

'It was so corrupt,' she said, 'bribing people for votes with empty promises, promises no politician could possibly keep. Government isn't just a group of men and women making decisions for the good of their own home town, there are so many other things to consider. Like the economy, and what other countries expect and accept of them. I've never pretended to understand fully

150

the complexity of government, but there was one thing I understood very clearly. It was when my ex-husband was about to speak in the House of Commons about raising old-age pensions. I suggested he should surprise everyone and speak about raising child benefit, or granting more money for education in primary schools, or children's hospitals. Do you know what that snake said to me?'

Darcy had no idea.

'He said, children don't vote. That statement told me something about him that frightened me. It took me a week to pluck up the courage, but when he went finally to make his speech about old-age pensions, I packed the Bentley and left. I've never spoken to him since. He sends me money for the boys, they're his heirs, and I know he wants them back, but he'll not get them. He'd send them away to public school and pay a nanny to look after them in the holidays, or worse. They're my sons too and I'm going to see that at least while they're young they have the freedom they deserve, freedom of mind as well as physical freedom.' She looked up at Darcy as if asking for approval and he saw there were tears in her eyes.

'You've made a great sacrifice for your children,' he said gently.

'No, I don't think so; remember, I happened to set myself free too.'

Kate was not only pretty: Darcy now saw that she was honest. He pushed all his previous doubts as far as he could to the back of his mind.

As the day faded and darkness took over, Kate went into the kitchen to find something in the little freezer to eat. 'We'd better eat inside, behind closed shutters,' she suggested. 'That way, if anything happens at the house opposite, no one'll be aware of us being here. Just leave the shutters open a crack so at least we can cast an eye from time to – Darcy!'

She'd gone white. In her hand was a long thin stiletto

151

dagger. There were ominous-looking dull brown marks on the slim blade.

'I – I trod on something, so I bent down to pick it up,' she stammered, holding the knife out to him. 'What the hell is it? Or shouldn't I ask?'

'I think, Kate,' Darcy replied slowly, taking the knife and wrapping it carefully in a clean handkerchief, 'you've just found our murder weapon.'

21

Pel was still wondering about the kidnapping. It was very odd and he was sure that the fact that there were no bullet holes, no scuff marks in the driveway, no blood, in fact no evidence at all, should tell him something important. He was also sure that Madame Barrau hadn't invented the incident. She was a nosy-parker and a peasant, but he doubted that she would have had enough imagination to make the whole thing up to attract attention to herself. And anyway, she'd been through what happened a dozen times with various officers, as well as with the boring Judge Brisard, and her story never wavered: it was the same simple clear account of witnessing a kidnapping as it had been when she'd first told it to Pel. But Margay had put up no resistance, apparently – he'd even had time to lock his vast oak front door. That was a new one. Unless . . . Of course! One of the oldest tricks in the book! Create a diversion to take attention away from the real crime. It was so obvious. Madame Barrau had been so conveniently stationed at the bottom of the drive to see everything. Had she just happened to be there? Or had they waited deliberately to see her coming down the hill to work, locked the front door, out of habit, he supposed, and staged the kidnapping with lots of shouting and shooting for her benefit, finally roaring off past her and almost knocking the poor woman in the ditch just to make sure she'd noticed? Madame Barrau had been completely taken in.

So had Pel, for that matter.

It was time to take advantage of Margay's disappearance and have a closer look at his house. He knew the Chief wouldn't like the idea, but he was going to have to get used to it.

To his surprise the Chief protested less vehemently than Pel had expected, finally signing the request for a search warrant.

'I suppose now that Margay's been whipped from under our fingertips it's a reasonable request. But Pel,' he said, 'please be careful. Don't break anything.'

'I'd better leave Annie Saxe behind, then.'

In fact it was Annie Saxe and de Troq' who accompanied Pel to Margay Manor with the search warrant. They'd telephoned ahead to Madame Barrau, asking her to wait for them with the keys to the front door.

She opened the door as instructed and they entered the house, all carefully wiping their feet before stepping on to the thick pile carpet.

'Why do Americans and British have carpet all over a house?' Pel complained. 'It's worse than walking through a ploughed field. It makes my legs ache.'

Madame Barrau gave them a guided tour, starting upstairs with the bedrooms and bathrooms. 'They must wash a lot,' Pel commented after seeing each of the five bedrooms and the five *en suite* bathrooms. 'Most houses only have one.'

'My parents didn't have any at all until I was seven,' Annie said. 'We lived outside the town and the only water we had was pumped up from a well. Plenty of peasants still live like that even nowadays.'

Madame Barrau agreed, adding that it was only when Margay took over the property that they had had a proper bathroom installed. 'And that's the door to the attic,' she finished, as they passed along the landing to go back downstairs.

On the ground floor Pel and de Troq' saw the modern kitchen equipped with microwave oven, indoor barbecue, eye-level grill, electric toaster, into which Pel noticed a slice of baguette would never fit, automatic rôtisserie – and so it went on. Madame Barrau took great delight in explaining all the gadgets and their uses; it was her domain and she was proud of it. At last they passed into the grand *salon* complete with fake porcelain leopards on either side of the fireplace, then back into the entrance hall and across into Margay's office on the opposite side. Although they carefully poked about in the papers sitting on the large leather-topped desk they discovered nothing. Opposite was an enormous chesterfield stacked with ugly embroidered cushions in startling colours.

'I reckon that's the most valuable thing in the house,' de Troq' remarked quietly, pointing at the chesterfield. 'If it's genuine, of course.'

As they left the office Madame Barrau directed them down the hall, saying there was another bathroom at the end, and after that just a couple of storerooms that were always locked.

They looked quickly into the bathroom, not believing there was any need for a sixth, and were waiting to be let into the storerooms when Madame explained that she didn't have the keys. She'd never been into the rooms since Margay had arrived.

It sounded interesting.

'I'm afraid we're going to have to see inside,' Pel pointed out firmly.

'Monsieur Margay is the only one with the keys to the doors,' she replied, 'and anyway, there are only old clothes and bits of unwanted furniture in there.'

'How do you know, if you've never been in there?'

'Monsieur told me.'

'Find a screwdriver, de Troq'. We'll have to take the door handles off and get in that way.'

'But you can't.'

Pel pulled himself up to his full height, which wasn't much, but at least it made him feel taller than the bleating Madame Barrau.

'I'm afraid, Madame,' he said, 'we must.'

Annie Saxe appeared behind them while they were still debating the subject. In her hands she was holding a screwdriver and a saw.

'What in the name of God have you been up to?' Pel looked alarmed. He didn't trust Annie further than he could see her, and it occurred to him that for the second half of their guided tour he hadn't seen her at all.

'I went up to the attic to have a quick look,' she answered calmly. 'I found these up there. I found something else, but I'll tell you about that later. Did you want me to unscrew a door knob?'

Within seconds she had the locked door knob off and was gently pushing open the storeroom door. This girl had hidden talents, Pel thought. What in hell's name can't she do?

To their disappointment the storeroom contained, as Madame Barrau had said, only old clothes and unwanted furniture.

'You see,' she said smugly, but before she could continue Pel cut her short and sent Annie to work on the second door.

Again they stepped inside. This time however, they found a desk, less elaborate than the one in Margay's official office, and a number of chairs. On the desk was a telephone together with a computer console and screen. There was a small table alongside containing a video machine and on the opposite wall was the largest television Pel had ever seen.

There was nothing else apart from the inevitable knee-deep carpet on the floor. There were no locked filing cabinets to open, no pictures behind which they might find a safe. Nothing, not even a window. The desk drawers weren't locked, but they were empty.

As they left, Madame Barrau carefully reset the alarm and locked the door after them. Annie handed her the tools she'd found in the attic. The door knobs and locks had been carefully replaced by her so that no one could accuse the police of damaging private property. Pel was satisfied he'd found what he'd been looking for. Computers and videos, everyone had them. Now he was sure. The locked office was empty of papers or cassettes; they'd obviously moved out to another place to conclude their business.

As they drove back through the countryside towards the city he sat in silence, mulling it over. There was still something missing but at least the pieces of the puzzle were coming together to make a slightly clearer picture.

'Sir?' Annie said from the back of the car.

He ignored her and went on with his process of thinking, sorting out facts and discarding unnecessary information.

'Sir?'

'Yes, what is it?' he snapped, irritated by the interruption.

'I know how they got in.'

'Jolly good.' Pel wasn't listening.

'Patron,' de Troq' said, 'Annie says she knows how they got in. I'd certainly like to hear what she has to say.'

Pel suddenly came to. 'Yes, yes. Of course, carry on, Annie, tell me, how did they get in?'

'I went up to the attic,' she explained. 'It was the only place we hadn't visited upstairs, and you'd be surprised what you find in people's attics. It can tell you a lot about a person, a bit like the books he reads.'

'Well?' Pel's patience was already wearing thin.

'I thought at first there was nothing up there except for cobwebs. Then I found the tools, just inside the door.

157

I think someone had put them there thinking they might be needed to remove the door knob to get out of the attic on to the landing had the door been locked.'

'What are you getting at, Annie? For the love of God, come to the point.'

'Having found the tools, I thought I'd better have a thorough look round. There's electricity at the top of the loft stairs so this time I switched the light on. To one side there was a pile of roofing tiles. They were stacked neatly under a large piece of stout cardboard fitted into the wooden planks of the roof.'

'So?'

'That's how they got in. Through the roof.'

'Through the roof!'

Annie was unimpressed by the sensation she had caused. 'Through the roof,' she repeated. 'It's very simple really, if you think about it, specially with houses roofed in the traditional way with curved tiles, which Margay Manor is. A ladder gets you up to the roof on the outside. You lift a dozen tiles or so – they are only laid one on top of the other, they're not fixed to anything.'

'Just a minute.' Pel was doubtful. 'How do you know how a house is built?'

'I helped my brothers reroof an old farmhouse of my aunt's.' Wonders would never cease. 'Anyway,' she continued, 'underneath you've got the *volige*, rough wooden planks, nailed to the main roof beams, at either end, but they don't even touch in the middle, you can easily get your hand between them. Take a saw and cut a section of planking out, then all you have to do is climb through the hole into the attic. You'd be in the house in a matter of minutes. The screwdriver I found was to unlock or dismantle the door furniture if indeed the attic door had been locked, and after that off you go and collect the goodies.'

'But he left by the kitchen door,' Pel pointed out, 'so who repaired the roof with the cardboard?'

'A second man.' Annie seemed sure of what she was saying. 'Once the first man is in and gives the signal, the second man goes up the ladder, stacks most of the removed tiles inside the attic, manipulates a sturdy bit of cardboard into place and covers it with the tiles he has left, just enough to make it look right from the outside. No one would notice until it rained hard and the cardboard collapsed. He goes down the ladder, puts it back in the barn, or in their own vehicle, and waits by the back door for the goodies to be handed out.'

'Why were there no footprints from the attic then? In fact no footprints anywhere.'

'Because when he got into the attic the first man took off his shoes and left them there, going into the house itself in his stockinged feet.'

'So where are these shoes?'

'In my handbag. I found them behind the door to the landing after coming down the attic stairs.' Even Pel was stunned into silence.

'I reckon', she went on, 'that the second man never went into the house – he just waited by the back door to be handed what the first man passed to him. Hence there was nothing heavy or large enough to require two men to manoeuvre it. The first man didn't leave the house until the job was finished; then he went out by the back door, locking it behind him and throwing the key into the bushes. He went to the loaded van parked in the drive without shoes, a small price to pay when they'd made such a good haul.'

De Troq' had slowed the car right down. They were entering the city limits as Pel turned in his seat to look at Annie Saxe, the Lion of Belfort, sitting demurely on the back seat, her haversack-sized handbag at her side.

'Is there more?' he asked seriously.

'A bit,' she said. 'Not much.'

'Pull over, de Troq', I'd like a drink. And I think', he

added, smiling his dyspeptic smile, 'the young lady sitting behind me has earned one too.'

They installed themselves outside a small bar as it filled up with workmen on their way home. The day had been blazing hot and the barman was doing a roaring trade. It was noisy, full of the smell of Gauloises, pastis and wine, mixed with the slightly less pleasant smell of perspiring bodies and stale urine – someone had left the door to the *pissoirs* open. The workmen seemed immune, however, and outside on the scruffy little terrace Pel, de Troq' and Annie were too far away to be aware of it. Annie, however, was causing a minor sensation. It wasn't often a woman found her way into this particular bar and if she did she was well known for her trade and looked the part. The workmen eyed Annie's young natural face and her slim legs stretched out beneath the table. As they went past one after another to stand at the bar the comments were becoming audible and de Troq' was making ready to defend the lady's honour. He needn't have bothered. The next raucous comment came and the man went sprawling. De Troq' noticed Annie withdraw a slender leg just in time to realise what had happened.

The muttering from inside had turned to applause. As the barman appeared to serve their beers he beamed at them. 'On the house,' he said. 'That's quite a little lady you've got there.' He beamed again at her and turned back towards the crowd inside.

'When you do something, Annie,' Pel said warmly, 'you certainly make an impression on people.'

'I'm not all that big, sir, but my brothers taught me how to look after myself. For that I'm very grateful.' She said it without conceit, simply stating a fact.

'Now back to work,' Pel said having taken a good suck at his beer. As he lit a cigarette he enveloped them both in a swirling blue cloud. 'Tell us the rest, Annie.'

'It's not much, but it might be important.'

'Go on, I'm all ears.'

'When I unscrewed the door knob on the first door it left a mark on the paintwork underneath, plus four small holes where the screws had been. The door had been painted without the lock, as is usual with professional painters, and the door knob was put on after the paint was dry. On the second door, however, the room that turned out to be the office, when I removed the door knob, it too left a mark, but inside that was a second mark, together with eight screw holes, four inside four others.'

'Which means that it had recently been replaced.'

'Which means, I think,' de Troq' put in, 'that our friend Bargiacchi got into that room too.'

'And found papers or cassettes he shouldn't have found.'

De Troq' recalled that Pierre had passed him a paper just before he'd left Château Coste.

'Bargiacchi's brother gave me something he found at the cottage. It was a sheet of paper covered with a sort of code. It didn't make any sense to him or to me, but I've given it to Debray, our computer expert, to see what he makes of it. It may just turn out to have great significance.'

Could this be the missing link?

22

Darcy and Kate were sitting side by side in the dark
behind the almost closed shutters, watching for signs of
life across the river. The stiletto knife, carefully wrapped,
had been pushed out of sight, but definitely not out of
their minds. They'd managed to cook themselves not a
bad meal and as they finished the dregs of a bottle of
eau-de-vie de prune, a strong and invigorating alcohol,
Darcy discovered that Kate smoked.

'It's rare,' she explained, 'that I actually feel the need for
the weed now. I used to smoke like a chimney when I lived
in the mausoleum up on the Scottish border. I must have
had insides like an ashtray. I suppose it was the boredom
or the loneliness.'

'Surely you're not bored or lonely now?'

'Hell, no, I'm not bored, not by a long chalk, and loneliness is something I've grown accustomed to. I wear it
like a friendly old cardigan. I like being alone.'

'And how do you like being with me?' Darcy asked as he
leant casually towards her in the hope of stealing a small
but meaningful kiss on the cheek.

'Darcy!' Sitting upright suddenly, Kate was staring at
the nearly closed shutters. 'There are lights across the
river.'

Darcy forgot the stolen kiss immediately and went
to peer through the crack of an opening they'd left.
Headlamps were approaching the house opposite.

'I'm going out to see if I can hear anything.'

He pushed open the wooden shutters and climbed silently out into the garden. As Kate followed they realised the headlamps belonged to a large vehicle, a lorry, that stopped some way from the house itself. In the headlamps of the lorry they could quite clearly see a number of men unloading crates and carrying them across to an open door.

'There are markings on those crates,' Darcy whispered. 'Find me the binoculars.'

Kate asked no questions but slid back into the cottage to hand him the pair of binoculars a moment later.

They watched in silence, hoping to catch what was being said – a name, a place, an accent even – but the men opposite weren't saying a word. They just went back and forth carrying the large crates until the lorry was apparently empty. They heard a heavy door slam and the rattle of keys in a large lock, then the men disappeared into the back of the lorry, leaving the driver alone in the cab where he had been all through the operation. The engine roared into life and the lorry was manoeuvred with difficulty to face back down the narrow track that had brought it to the house. Slowly the headlamps disappeared among the trees.

'Shame we can't follow them,' Kate said, still in a hushed voice.

Darcy didn't reply but went on listening to the sound of the retreating vehicle. As the river bank fell silent once again he climbed back through the window of the cottage and beckoned to Kate to follow. When they were both inside he quietly closed the shutters and switched on the light.

'You don't think there's anyone still across there, do you?' she whispered.

'No, but I can't be sure. If we can hide without showing our lights so could they. I intend to keep watch.'

As Darcy made himself comfortable by the window Kate busied herself with making coffee.

'Did you see the markings on the crates?' Darcy asked as he took the glass of coffee she offered him.

'They looked oriental to me.'

'They were, but there was also another, one which might interest your father. Or rather two – two small cats' heads, two smiling cats' heads.'

The Hôtel de Police was full of people as Pel and Nosjean pushed their way through to the staircase.

'Anything for us, Chief Inspector?'

Pel turned to see Sarrazin, the freelance journalist, waving his notebook above his head at him.

'Nothing new,' Pel replied, 'but if you hang on I'll send someone down with a full description of Margay. You could put that in the papers if you like.'

'Good on you!' Sarrazin called back.

Pel frowned. He continued frowning until he was safely behind the closed door of his office. At least there it was peaceful.

He knew it wouldn't last long and it didn't. The door reopened almost immediately to reveal Annie Saxe carrying a cup of coffee for him.

'Decaffeinated,' she announced as she put it on the desk in front of her boss. 'And there's a telex from London.'

As she disappeared he picked up the telex. It was from Goschen to let Pel know that Charles L. Incks was due to leave London for Toulouse that morning. Interesting, Pel thought. Perhaps he should get Darcy to meet him at the airport.

Darcy, however, was no longer at the château. A rather flustered young woman introduced herself as Jo-jo and explained that Darcy and Kate had not yet returned from the cottage by the river, and they'd been there all night. Darcy was up to his old tricks again – he must be feeling better. Pel was just allowing a smile to creep across his face at the thought of Darcy's old tricks when Nosjean came through the office door like a small explosion.

'Doing impressions of the Chief?' Pel asked, making a rare attempt at humour.

'Sorry, patron, Annie Saxe was coming down the corridor like a whirlwind. I thought it best to get out of her way as fast as I could.'

'She has that effect, but a couple of corners of her brain work on overdrive, so we'll just have to put up with her.'

'Point taken.' Nosjean was inclined to agree with Pel's summary of the Lion of Belfort. 'The document that de Troq' gave to Debray, patron,' he went on. 'It's got him baffled, he says it's too technical for him, so he's faxing it to the experts in Paris hoping they'll come up with the answers. In the mean time, I thought I should remind you that tonight's the night of Vlaxi's extravaganza. It's the fourteenth of July.'

With all the enquiries they had on their plate, not just the two murders and the Margay robbery, but also a couple of thousand other minor problems all requiring attention, Pel hadn't even noticed the date. It made no difference to him – bank holiday or no bank holiday, nothing had changed in his department. While everyone else in France was sleeping late his policemen were all present and correct. Pel in particular. What a life!

'Darras has volunteered to watch,' Nosjean was saying. 'So has Annie. I'm going to let her go – if you agree, of course. If things do turn nasty it might be wise to have a woman present. There are bound to be women among the guests, unless of course Vlaxi doesn't do that either.'

'Are you going?'

'Naturally.'

'Good, that should be enough. I'll leave it up to you to get the thing set up. If I'm needed I'll be on the end of the phone. Don't hesitate. If in doubt, ring me, this could be important. Make sure you know where de Troq' is going

165

to be, and', he finished with glee, 'tell Misset to wait up, just in case.'

As Nosjean was half-way through the door he turned to add another piece of information. 'They've found the car that sped Margay away.'

'Inform me.'

'Black Mercedes, not his own, not as big. It was abandoned just before the entrance to the Sunshine Motorway leading south.'

'That doesn't surprise me,' Pel said. 'Who does it belong to?'

'A businessman on the other side of the city. He reported it stolen the day of the kidnapping, but only to his local gendarmerie. He has a reputation for leaving his car where it shouldn't be and taking a taxi home. He temporarily lost his licence some years ago for drunken driving and takes no chances now. The gendarmerie treated the reported theft as a bit of a joke. Thought he'd simply had a few too many and couldn't remember.'

'Get over there and stir them up a bit. It sounds to me as if they don't take life seriously enough. I don't suppose they'll be able to tell you anything, but you'd better ask all the same. Before you leave, organise an *avis de recherche*, an all-points bulletin, on Margay. That, together with the description in the newspapers, might turn him up, although I rather suspect he's well and truly gone into hiding for the time being, thinking he's safely out of the way. But we'd better play his game. If he sees the newspapers are still interested he'll know we are too. It'll lull him into a false sense of security thinking that his kidnapping fooled us – that way he'll have the confidence to go ahead with whatever it is he's been planning, and I've got a good idea where that'll be. We'll just have to wait for him to make the next move. Whatever you do, don't breathe a word of what we're really thinking to anyone. Especially Misset. You know what he's like – worse than Madame Barrau for gossip.' For a long time he'd suspected

Misset of passing information to the press to earn a bit of pocket money, and while nothing had been proved, it was wise not to take chances.

Pel took all his files down the corridor to confer with the Chief and keep him informed as to their activities. The Chief, however, was worried.

'There's still something missing,' he said. 'All these things connect up, that's for sure. But why? For a racket in videos and computer games? It doesn't seem enough. Even if the videos were pornographic, we're fairly broad-minded on the subject in France. If people want to see a dirty movie all they've got to do is tune into *Canal Plus* on the television late on Saturday night, or I should say Sunday morning, and they've got tits and bums bursting out of the screen at them. If it's for the newly released films, I can't see there being much of a market for them, except for a few private clubs. That area of the market is fairly well sewn up. Most people won't touch them – they prefer to wait for the film to be officially released on cassette and hire it from their local video club. Which leaves the computer games. Are they really that profitable?'

Pel went back to his own office and meticulously considered all the information they had so far. The solution had to be there somewhere. It was staring him in the face, he knew: he just had to find it hidden in one of the dozens of reports.

The phone rang on his desk, interrupting his train of thought.

'*Merde,*' he said out loud as he answered.

'Same to you too, patron. Darcy here.'

'Darcy! What have you got?'

'A sore arse and legs that are killing me.'

'I beg your pardon?'

'I spent most of yesterday and this morning in the saddle,' Darcy explained.

'It'll do you good.' Pel was smiling to himself: Darcy seemed to have met his match at long last. 'It wasn't so long ago that you spent most of your spare time bed-hopping between girlfriends. Perhaps mounting a horse will calm you down a bit.'

'I'm calmed. Extremely calmed, as calm as could be, but bloody stiff too. When I woke up this morning, alone I might add, zipped like a virgin into my single sleeping bag, I could hardly move. Kate was as agile as usual. Do you think the agony wears off after you get the hang of it?'

'Like anything, I'm sure you'll get used to it in the end.'

Their exchange was good-natured and friendly and Pel was delighted to find Darcy back to his normal self. However, he hoped there was more to report than a simple pain in the arse.

'Last night we kept watch and a lorry turned up. We couldn't see the driver, he never got down from the cab, and the other men, four of them, were just silhouettes in the headlamps. There was no talking either, it was as if they'd taken a vow of silence like Trappist monks, but what we did see was the crates. Quite a number of them, seven in all, and all with the same markings. I can't tell you any names because it looked like Chinese writing to me, but there was one thing that caught my eye and that was a small drawing stamped on each of the crates.'

'Well, what was it, for God's sake?'

'Two grinning cats' heads.'

The Catmen, there it was again. The Professor had certainly stumbled on to something in Hong Kong: if only they could find out for sure what the hell it was.

'Oh, and patron, another thing, I think our murder weapon's turned up. Kate trod on it yesterday evening. It's a stiletto and there are what look like bloodstains still on it.'

'Sounds like what we're looking for. Get it up here to Forensics immediately.'

'Do you want me to bring it personally?'

'Of course I do, and now!'

'I thought you would. My flight leaves at 1400. They'll have it later this afternoon.'

So, another little clue had turned up, but in the wrong place. Unless Georges Bargiacchi was the murderer and had taken the weapon with him when he went south. He hoped Leguyader would find something. If there was blood on it, the chances were that it would be from the old lady, Madame Marty, or from Lulu Lafon – as far as he was concerned, either would do. That, together with a couple of neat fingerprints, could wrap the case up. But that would be asking for miracles and, as Pel knew only too well, miracles were very rare in police work.

Darcy left him to brood over the information he'd given him. As he put the phone back into its cradle he saw that Kate watching him.

'I'll drive you to Albi airport,' she said quietly, 'in the Bentley if you like.'

23

The night of Vlaxi's party, the fourteenth of July. While the whole of France was dancing and singing and letting off fireworks, Pel sat beside the phone waiting for something to happen. His wife knew him well enough to leave him with a small whisky while she listened to Bach, well turned down, on the record player. Madame Routy had been banished to her own rooms and instructed to keep the television turned down to merely loud.

Someone had had the bright idea of putting Annie Saxe into a smart black dress and ringing Vlaxi to ask if he'd thought of having a private photographer at his glamorous party. He hadn't, and welcomed the idea gladly. Before Pel had left the office he'd seen Annie in her photographer's outfit and had to admit she looked the part.

'For God's sake keep an eye on her,' he'd said to Nosjean. 'She thinks she knows how to look after herself, but she's only small, and the rugby tackles her brothers taught her won't be much good up against a group of gangsters all armed to the teeth like Rambo.'

The team had reassured him, but sitting by the phone that evening he was still worried. He'd grown strangely attached to the little Lion of Belfort and didn't want Vlaxi to get his filthy hands on her.

The hours ground past and still there was no news. He contacted the Hôtel de Police, but the sergeant on duty confirmed there was nothing to report. He went on turning the current cases over in his mind, trying not to think about the party. The two murders, the robbery, the kidnapping, Bargiacchi's disappearance, the messages from Professor Henri, Incks arriving from London . . . Where was it all leading?

Just before two o'clock Pel allowed his wife to persuade him to retire. She touched his sleeve. 'Come to bed now, *mon cher*. If they need you, they'll ring. There's a phone by the bed, after all – it's not as if you won't hear it.'

He reluctantly followed her up the stairs, knowing she was right, but he couldn't rest. Finally he switched the light back on and dialled the Hôtel de Police one more time.

'Nosjean just called in,' he was told. 'The party's still in full swing, lots of eating, drinking and making merry, but so far nothing to merit police intervention. They're just watching and growing bored.'

'Annie Saxe, any news of her?'

'Yes, she came out just after midnight, with two reels full of snapshots. She went home to change, but is back with the boys on surveillance now.'

Pel settle back at last, realising he'd lost at least three hours' sleep for nothing. What an anti-climax!

The following morning a number of things happened to change Pel's mind.

Leguyader was the first visitor to his office.

'It's not what we expected,' he told Pel.

'What is it then?' Pel was in no mood to be patient with the walking encyclopedia.

'Who is it? That's going to be your next question, and that I'm afraid I can't tell you. There were traces of blood on the blade of the stiletto knife, as Darcy pointed out when he brought it to me, but they are from neither Madame Marty nor Lulu Lafon. Marty's blood group was A positive, and Lafon's was O positive. The blood on the knife is a negative group, so I think you'll be looking at a third murder before long. However, one thing is sure, the knife is the weapon that killed the two women – either that one or one that is identical. For the moment that's all I can tell you, except that there were no fingerprints.'

Pel stared after the disappearing Leguyader. Holy Mother of God! Another body to look forward to.

A great deal of excitement came through the door with Nosjean and Annie Saxe.

'Patron! Look at this!'

They handed over a pile of photographs that had just come back from being developed in the photographic department. There were a number of surprises among Vlaxi's guests. The local Member for the Opposition, for instance, talking to the estranged wife of a well-known councillor. Degusse was there too, the lawyer who had dealt with Tagliatti, the gangster, before he'd been assassinated. It looked very likely that, together with Tagliatti's operations, Vlaxi had taken over his lawyer as well. There were also the inevitable less public faces that could be found on the police files, but that was no surprise. The real surprise was the photograph Annie Saxe finally placed on Pel's desk.

'Margay!'

'That's what we said,' Nosjean agreed.

'Didier isn't so sure,' Annie added.

'He does look better out of his dreadful cowboy suit. I admire his taste in evening dress,' Pel commented, looking closely at the photo. 'Very discreet and upper class.' He was surprised to see him there at all, because he remembered Vlaxi saying Margay was a snob and had declined his invitation, but there he was, visible behind a crowd of people. Though he was in the distance and not perfectly in focus, Pel was convinced it was Margay.

'Get Didier in here,' he said.

Didier Darras appeared almost immediately as if he'd been lurking in the corridor waiting for the call.

'Is this Margay?'

'It could be,' the young man answered, 'but, well, I'm not sure.'

'Explain.'

'I spent a lot of time watching Margay Manor, and in doing so I got to know Margay, from a distance, extraordinarily well. If I listened to his voice, it would very likely mean nothing to me, but watching him walk and talk I'd recognise him anywhere. This Margay had a different manner about him.'

'He's put on different clothes for the party,' Pel pointed out.

'It's not just that.'

'Could he have affected a different manner to impress Vlaxi's friends?'

'It's possible, patron. I can't tell you any more than that, it's just a feeling I had watching through the binoculars. It didn't feel like Margay.'

Pel had always taken his team's hunches seriously. Sometimes they came to nothing, but often there was good reason behind them. Didier Darras was still fairly new to police work but he'd always used his brains. He was a calm young man, and not given to wild imagination. Pel considered what he'd said carefully and hung on to the photo to study.

If Margay had really been kidnapped he most certainly wouldn't be able, or allowed, to turn up at Vlaxi's party to celebrate Bastille Day in full evening dress. He'd be locked up somewhere good and tight or possibly even dead by now. If, however, the kidnap had only been a diversion, as he believed, surely Margay wouldn't risk showing himself back in the area at something as ostentatious as Vlaxi's celebrations – it was asking for trouble. It was true that they hadn't known they were under surveillance, or that the photographer was a policewoman, but all the same it was risky. Having staged his own abduction, surely Margay wouldn't have been so careless? And another thing, after initially refusing the invitation why had he turned up at all? Of course, Vlaxi could have been lying, but even so Margay's appearance at the house was very odd. Pel picked up the photo and studied it more closely. It certainly looked like Margay. Clothes changed a person's appearance dramatically. Changing from a cowboy outfit to a smart dark evening suit, for Margay the American, had certainly been dramatic.

Then Pel remembered something. He lifted the phone.

'Find me Darras again. I want to speak to him.'

Didier arrived back not long afterwards and stood in front of Pel's desk waiting to be questioned.

'When you were watching the Margay house,' Pel said carefully, 'you saw him leave dressed in an ordinary suit and tie?'

'Yes, patron.'

'Tell me about it.'

There was very little to tell but Didier obliged and went through what he'd seen again for Pel: just Margay arriving at his house dressed like a businessman and leaving some time later in the same clothes. That evening he was back in his cowboy outfit.

'Thank you, Didier, that's all I wanted to know.'

There was an idea nagging at the back of Pel's brain. He opened up the Margay robbery file and read Didier's report through again. Then, slamming it shut, he reached for the phone and began the nerve-racking operation of dialling London.

24

Nosjean and de Troq' had joined Darcy in his office after they'd lunched briefly at the Bar Transvaal. The three of them were comparing notes and trying to make sense of a lot of cases that seemed to make no sense at all. They too had been right through every file, pausing over details that had been unimportant, asking themselves if they'd missed something, but they came to the same conclusion: Georges Bargiacchi was the key. He was the man they suspected of robbing Margay Manor, and because of him, two women had been murdered, possibly to shut them up, or in an attempt to find him. He'd turned up at Kate Henri's house and begged the keys of a remote cottage and gone into hiding, but now there was no trace of him. They all agreed Bargiacchi had to be found.

They didn't have to wait long.

Darcy had gone along to see Pel, hoping he might have something to add and suggesting that he should return to the Tarn that afternoon and bring pressure to bear on Bargiacchi's half-brother, Pierre. Darcy felt he knew much more than he was telling, and was trying to protect Georges. If this wasn't the case, and he firmly believed it was, then at least Pierre would have the best idea as to where Georges had gone. They had to prise something from his memory.

Pel nodded. 'All right, Darcy, get back down there. Try his wife too,' he added.

'Jo-jo?'

'Yes. See if you can persuade Kate to work on her. Often a woman can wheedle something out of another woman when in front of a man her mouth stays tightly shut. If not, revert to brute force on both her and her husband.'

Darcy was none too keen on either idea but he was at least willing to try.

'Okay. I'll get Kate to meet me from Albi airstrip.'

Pel was about to open his mouth to make a suitably cutting remark about Darcy and his women when he was stopped by the clanging of bells. He lifted the receiver.

'Annie here, sir. I have Lady-Kate-Henri-Smythe on the line for Inspector Darcy. Is he with you?' She hadn't quite got the name right, but she got full marks for trying.

Kate was agitated. 'Something terrible's happened,' she told Darcy. 'They've found Georges.'

As he listened Darcy flipped a switch on the phone so that Kate's voice was audible to Pel through a small loudspeaker. 'They've found Bargiacchi,' he repeated for Pel's benefit. 'That's not terrible,' he replied to Kate.

'Yes it is. He's dead.'

'How?'

'A hunting accident, they say, but I don't believe it for a minute. Should I go to the police here and tell them what I know? Pierre doesn't want me to – he wants to talk to you.'

'Hang on, Kate,' Darcy said gently. 'Start at the beginning. Who found him? And where?'

'Radio Itzac, Laurel and Hardy – you know, the two scruffy old peasants. They'd been out poaching around the cottage – poking around more likely, after we'd reroused their interest, you know what they're like – and as they came back along the forest track they found Georges' body. When I say forest track, it's not one in general use, but one made by deer or boar. They tend to keep to the undergrowth like the animals, that way they catch more. But this time they caught something they weren't expecting. Blasé virtually fell over him. Raffi thought Blasé had been at the bottle surreptitiously, but finally went to pick up his spreadeagled friend. It was then they realised who'd tripped him up. It was Georges and as dead as a dodo. Surprisingly they didn't touch him but came straight to tell me. Jo-jo was here and I think they half expected to find Pierre with her. They recognised Georges, you see – I don't think he'd been there long because in this heat, even in the shade of the forest . . .' Darcy and Pel knew only too well what the summer flies could do to a body.

'Anyway,' she went on, 'I rang the police and they went back into the forest with the two old boys to recover the body. Pierre came home at lunchtime to collect Jo-jo and I had to tell him. I got them to stay for lunch but he was weird, he didn't say a word and eventually got up from the table and went to identify the body. He came back later and told me they were considering it as a hunting accident – half the side of his face was missing from the blast of a shotgun. Accidents happen, you know what the *chasseurs* are like, shoot anything that moves, but the season isn't open, not that it stops some people. Pierre's acting strangely. He's forbidden me to go back to the local police and tell them about Georges' wanting to hide at the cottage and his involvement with your American's robbery. He says they're a load of corrupt *cons*, without a bloody brain between them. But, Darcy, someone's got to do something. They've hauled the two old boys in for questioning, they've taken their hunting guns too – I think they're going to accuse them. They were terrified. At the very least they'll be done for poaching. They've got no money to pay a fine, so they'll be sent to prison. Even if it's only for a week it'll kill them. Darcy, what do I do? Everyone's asking me to help them and I don't know how.'

'Tell her you're on your way,' Pel said.

When he'd put the phone down Darcy looked across

the desk at Pel. 'I don't think it was a hunting accident, either. I think we've just found the third dead body Leguyader warned you about.'

'Get down there on the next flight, Darcy, and tell their forensic man to look for a stiletto wound in the neck,' Pel said. 'I'm sure they aren't as brainless as Pierre suggests, but they don't know what to look for. We do. Keep an eye on Pierre, too: we don't want him doing anything stupid. He could stumble into our other cases and ruin our chances of concluding them satisfactorily.'

'I'll get Laurel and Hardy released too, if I can. A night under *garde à vue* would be terrible for them. And anyway, who'd put the chicken back on the fridge if she fell off?'

Darcy left Pel scratching his head and wondering what the hell he'd meant.

When Darcy arrived at Albi that evening on the TAT flight from Paris, Kate ran across the tarmac towards him. To his surprise and delight she flung her arms round his neck.

'Thank goodness you're back. I've been frantic with worry,' she said. Darcy, not one to miss an opportunity, dropped his bag and pulled her towards him. 'Don't worry,' he said, 'we'll sort it all out.' But Kate wriggled free, already telling him another piece of disturbing news.

'Pierre's gone.'

'Oh no! When?'

'He took off this afternoon, saying he had something important to do. He's not come back yet. Jo-jo's almost hysterical. She keeps bursting into tears and shouting at the boys. She's drinking too, I don't know what to do with her. It'll be getting dark soon. I think I'll have to keep her at the house tonight – I can't send her home if Pierre's done a bunk.'

'Never mind about them now,' Darcy said swinging his bag into the back of the open Bentley. 'Take me to the Hôtel de Police, I might just catch the Forensic lab still open. Let's hope they haven't all gone home. I'd like to get Laurel and Hardy out tonight if I can.'

Unexpectedly Kate leant over and planted a kiss on Darcy's cheek. If the statement was worth a peck on the cheek, what would the action be worth? He was suddenly impatient to have the two old men set free.

It took some doing but Darcy and Kate finally made their way to the Forensic lab. The inspector at the Hôtel de Police was at first none too willing to give permission, but after a quick phone call to Pel, who explained the situation to the Chief in Albi, they were on their way.

They found the pathologist, Monsieur Guy Roques, sitting in a small white-painted office, filling in forms. As they entered he looked up at them and removed a pair of glasses with lenses as thick as the bottoms of wine bottles.

'Yes? What do you want?' He squinted at them.

'I'm Inspector Darcy of –'

'Oh, yes, yes. I've been expecting you, they rang through and told me you were on your way. Now do sit down and tell me all about it.' He was a fussy little man with wisps of fawn hair hanging haphazardly around his temples, but he was helpful and more than willing to listen.

'Well, well,' he said, sucking the end of a biro and managing to daub blue ink all over his lips. 'Very interesting. I think we'd better have a look. I certainly didn't notice anything odd when I did my autopsy, but then I wasn't looking for it, was I? I thought I was studying just another hunting accident, you know – that's what it looked like to me. A bit out of season, I suppose, but it does happen from time to time. I've seen lots of hunting accidents. The moment October arrives they start wheeling them in.' He made it sound as if dead bodies arrived in his laboratory by the lorry load, but he was quite cheerful about it.

'Perhaps we should examine the body together?' he suggested, getting up from his chair and scattering forms and files all over the floor. Kate knelt to help pick them up. 'That's right, dear,' Roques said, 'you collect them up while we go next door. It's no place for a young lady.'

He patted her gently on the head as he passed, like an amiable old grandfather, and led Darcy through into the next room where they both put on long white jackets. Roques collected the body of Bargiacchi from the vast refrigerator and pushed him on a trolley into the examination room. There was a label hanging from one toe with his name and the date on it. One side of his face was badly damaged, looking like a discarded lump of meat in a butcher's shop. Roques slipped his thin plastic gloves over his slim hands and started the examination.

'I never start in the obvious place. Sometimes it makes you jump to conclusions and you miss something. But it seems as if I did all the same, *n'est ce pas?*' He smiled humbly at Darcy before going on. 'I always start as far away from the major wound as possible. It's very interesting what I find sometimes, and how it changes my final report. However, having slipped up this time, I shan't bore you with all the finer details. We'll go straight to the head and neck. The right side is almost untouched, as you can see, but here on the left – well, you can see for yourself, it's not very pretty, but I think what you're looking for will be hidden here, if it's here at all, of course.'

It was well over half an hour later that they came back into the office where Kate was patiently waiting in front of a newly stacked neat pile of files.

'Well?'

'Found it, my dear. It was well disguised by the blast of a gun, a nine-millimetre rifle. One might say it was a deliberate attempt to confuse me. However, once I knew what I was looking for, it was relatively easy. I'm most grateful to you, Inspector Darcy. I've learnt something today.' He shook them both by the hand and went back to sorting his forms.

As a result of their discovery the Chief, Commissaire

Calvet, agreed that there was little point in holding the two peasants any longer and ordered their immediate release. After a brief call to Pel to let him know what they'd found, they went downstairs to meet Laurel and Hardy. They shuffled out into the main hall looking like a pair of refugees who'd been on the road since last year, but their miserable faces cheered up the moment they noticed Kate and Darcy. Immediately they put their shuffle into top gear and hurried to shake his hand vigorously and give her prickly kisses on both cheeks as usual.

'You look as though you need a drink,' Darcy suggested.

They didn't object and followed them out to the Bentley, which was causing quite a stir outside the Préfecture next door. Darcy flipped out his badge to save having to answer a lot of silly questions and started pushing the old men into the back seat. 'But we'll dirty it,' they protested.

'It's only a car,' Kate reassured them.

They left the gendarmes, who'd been admiring the Bentley with their mouths hanging open.

'I think they'll be putting in applications for a transfer to Burgundy,' Darcy laughed as he swung the car out into the road. 'They obviously think policemen are very well paid up there.'

25

While Laurel and Hardy were happily installing themselves behind a good tot of pastis, watched by Kate and Darcy, Pel took Didier Darras to see Vlaxi. It was time to confront him with the photograph. When they got to the house, however, they found all the shutters closed and no one answering the bell on the gate.

'Do you think they're in there and just not wanting to come out?' Didier asked as he tried the intercom for a second time.

'I don't know,' Pel replied, 'but you're going to find out for me. Shin over the gates and have a quick look round.'

Didier did as he was told, coming back a few minutes later to report that there was no sign of life at all.

'So they've scarpered too,' Pel thought out loud. 'That was sudden.'

As Didier dropped to the ground beside him, Pel went on, 'When we get back I want an *avis de recherche* put out, but if Vlaxi is seen I don't want him stopped. I just want to know where he is.'

Now Pel knew that whatever it was they'd been planning was about to happen. Margay had gone from his house, Incks had arrived in France and Vlaxi had done a bunk. They must all be heading for the same place and for the moment he didn't want the hornets' nest disturbed. He was still waiting for Debray or Paris to decipher the document Pierre had given de Troq' before he'd left Château Coste.

He didn't have to wait long.

Debray came into his office early the following morning with his explanation.

'I couldn't make head nor tail of it so I faxed it to Paris. It had them baffled for a bit, too. Then I got an urgent call to join them in the Paris office and went up yesterday. My reception was a distinctly chilly one. I was dusting frost from my jacket most of the afternoon. They demanded to know where the hell I'd got the document. It's top secret.'

The phone went and Pel was obliged to be patient as he lifted the receiver. It was Darcy.

'Pierre's turned up. He's made a discovery, patron,' he announced. 'He broke into Incks' house last night.'

'Did he indeed? Inform me.'

'Instead of finding a nice little cosy holiday home, he found banks of electronic equipment and computers.'

'I thought he might.' Pel was already one jump ahead. 'Don't let Pierre out of your sight, Darcy. I'm coming down as fast as possible. Be at Albi airport to meet the Paris flight this afternoon.'

He replaced the receiver thoughtfully in its cradle and turned back to Debray. 'Now,' he said cheerfully, 'where were we?'

When the small jet touched down, Kate and Darcy stood side by side waiting for Pel. Darcy was not best pleased to see de Troq' follow him down the steps of the aircraft. He felt he was at last making headway with Kate. They'd spent a very pleasant evening together after they'd delivered the Radio Itzac double act to their tumbledown house. It hadn't been intimate by any means, particularly as they'd had to put the drunk Jo-jo to bed beside an equally pickled Pierre, but it had been surprisingly enjoyable, considering the problems that surrounded them. With the baron's arrival he suspected he wouldn't get the chance to inject into their relationship the intimacy that he'd hoped for. Kate would probably go galloping off into the sunset with de Troq'.

True to form, the baron took Kate's hand and kissed it while clicking his aristocratic heels. Darcy felt like clicking his aristocratic head against a couple of stout paving stones until he remembered they had a job to do and, graciously relieving Pel of his overnight bag, he directed them both to the car. Pel's eyes widened as he saw the Bentley but he refrained from saying anything, allowing himself to be driven back through the countryside covered with vineyards in the sinking sun to Château Coste.

Pierre was sitting on the terrace sullenly watching the four boys as they arrived. Jo-jo was nowhere to be seen; they suspected she was still in a darkened room nursing a thick head. Introductions were made by Darcy while Kate disappeared into the kitchen to prepare refreshments. They sat together at the large table quietly listening to what Pierre had to tell them about Incks' house.

While he finished his description, Pel studied him before he spoke. 'From the report I have,' he said slowly, 'the house is well and truly locked and shuttered. Not even the two old peasants known as Radio Itzac managed to find a way in. So how did you do it?'

'Through the roof. Easy when you know how!' But his satisfied smile didn't last for long.

'And did you leave your shoes in the attic just as you did at Margay Manor?'

Pierre looked quickly at Chief Inspector Pel. For a moment they all saw fear in his eyes, and Darcy half expected him to bolt through the open door. But his expression changed to being tired and completely beaten.

'Okay,' he sighed at last. 'No, I didn't leave my shoes in the attic. There was no thick carpet like at Margay

Manor. I'm done for, aren't I?' he asked sadly. 'But if it's of interest to you lot, it wasn't me in the attic, it was Georges, my brother. I was outside dealing with the ladder and taking what he handed me through the kitchen door. Oh, *merde*!' His head sank into his hands. Kate reached out and touched his arm.

'Perhaps if you tell them everything, Pierre, they might be able to help you,' she suggested.

'It's the clink for me,' he moaned. 'I know it, you know it. Oh, *putain*, what will become of Jo-jo and the boys?'

'Pierre, there is something you should know before you despair completely,' Pel interjected kindly. Both Darcy and de Troq' stared at the gentleness with which he spoke. This was a Pel they didn't recognise. 'This affair is far more important than a simple robbery. If you are able, by your information, to help us catch the men involved, it could stop a European scandal and another robbery of sorts but on a very large scale. Tell me what you know. The break-in at Margay Manor is, in fact, an insignificant detail, but without it we would never have discovered what Margay and his mates were planning.'

Pierre looked up, rubbing the back of his neck. He seemed with difficulty to be coming to a major decision. 'Georges was recruited by a firm up your way to do the air-conditioning installation at Margay's place,' he said at last. 'It was a good contract worth a lot of money and he was well pleased when he was paid in cash. When Margay moved in with his furniture all the workmen were invited to the house for aperitifs before they were paid. I think he was showing off and it set them talking. Unfortunately it set Georges thinking. He said the house was stuffed full of treasures. He knew the house inside out, he'd crawled all over the place soldering pipes and installing air ducts and blowers. He wanted to do it. I told him he was mad and turned him down three or four times until in the end he said he was going to do it anyway but with some other silly *con*. I was frightened for my brother – he's much younger than I am and when our mother died I was all he had left, he's almost like a son to me. I couldn't let him risk it with someone else, so in the end I realised I had to go along with him. There was no one else I trusted.

'Trouble was,' he sighed, 'although the *casse* went without a hitch, what we'd loaded into our van was rubbish. No one would touch it. In the end we had to dump it. But Georges didn't seem bothered, he waved a file of papers under my nose and told me to wait and see what that brought in. I didn't know what was in there, but I guessed he was going to have a go at blackmail. I told him he was crazy but again he laughed at me and off he went with his file.' He passed a hand wearily over his forehead. 'Then his landlady was murdered, and his bird, Lulu – mind you, she was a dreadful old cow, but the landlady was a sweet old dear.'

'Monsieur Marty died shortly afterwards,' Pel told him.

'Oh, God. We didn't know that. Anyway, Georges turned up down here. I'd only been away for twenty-four hours to do the job and try and sell the stuff we'd pinched, he'd been absent longer. When Kate told me he'd turned up I went to see him at the cottage. He was there for longer than we thought, but he's a sly one and climbed into the loft whenever anyone turned up. He was worried but still confident he could sell the papers back. He told me he had a meeting arranged. They must have done for him then.' He stopped talking for a moment to look at the policemen listening to him. 'I know I'm for it,' he said, 'and I'll take what's coming if I have to, but he was my brother, and I'll do anything to help you catch the bastards that killed him, even if it makes no difference to you sending me down.'

'Did you see any of the men across the river at Incks' house?'

'Only a bloke Georges said was called Margay.'

'Have you ever seen Incks himself?'

'Georges said it was the same man.'

186

'I don't think you'll find that is the case,' Pel said. 'I'm still waiting for confirmation from London but I'm fairly sure I've solved that bit of the puzzle. Margay turned up at a party just outside Dijon after he was supposed to have been kidnapped, but also after Incks arrived in France for an important conference in Toulouse.'

26

That evening Pel went to introduce himself to Commissaire Calvet, the Chief at Albi. A police car was sent for him and he was away until almost midnight.

After a long time on the phone Pel decided he'd done all he could for the time being. At least he had the answers to some of the key questions. At least he knew now what the whole mystery was about. Even Pel, who'd seen most things and was surprised by very few, thought it was quite a plan. In fact it was incredible.

Although the puzzle Professor Henri had sent from Hong Kong wasn't completely solved, Pel was now sure it was only a matter of time before they inevitably uncovered the final answers. What had he meant by 'Cats'? Charles L. Incks, or Lynx as he could be known, was very probably one, but the written word had been plural. Pel wasn't too worried though, feeling that it was perhaps just a code name for those involved in L. Incks' electronic wizardry.

During the course of their discussions, Pel and Calvet agreed that they would have preferred to keep the affair to themselves but, due to the gravity of the situation and its possible consequences, they both reluctantly had to admit that Interpol should be informed. Fortunately they were able to convince them that the situation was well under control and for the time being no outside involvement would be forced on them. For the time being.

Pel and Calvet felt they had done well, so far.

It was very late when Pel arrived back at the château. De Troq' had followed Pierre and Jo-jo home to sleep in their sitting-room by the front door and prevent Pierre from doing anything foolish, so it was Darcy who offered Pel a small cognac in the privacy of their rooms in the barn. At last Pel let Darcy in on what he was thinking and watched contentedly as Darcy's eyes grew wider.

It was early the following morning, when they all re-assembled for breakfast at the immense table in the kitchen of the château, that Pel treated the rest of them to the same information.

'They're identical twins, Margay and Incks. I got on to Goschen after we thought we'd seen Margay at Vlaxi's party. Didier Darras had seen Margay dressed differently arriving at and then leaving Margay Manor – curious, because if he lived there he should have left and come back to the house, not the other way round. He also saw someone we thought was Margay at the party but there was something odd about him – he said his manner was different. It made me think. Goschen had a search done at Somerset House, where the English keep their records of births, deaths and marriages, and yesterday he confirmed his findings. They are twins, born to a Miss Gladys Ball. She was unmarried and in those days, forty-seven years ago to be precise, it was still shameful – in any case, she had no means of supporting the two babies – so she put both boys up for adoption. One was adopted by the Incks family, a well-to-do couple who educated and brought up their son, Charles Lawrence, in a way that was expected of moneyed English people. He did well and ended up, as we know, as an attaché to a minister of the British government. The second of the twins was sadly never adopted, but went to an orphanage. As he grew up he became more and more difficult, finally running away at the age of fifteen. The orphanage tried to find him but they never saw him again. We now know he went

189

to America at some point and there eventually changed his name. He'd already been in trouble in England, and it looks as if he hasn't altered since he left. At some stage he discovered he had a twin and would have been delighted to know who and what he was. Goschen has done some discreet digging and uncovered the fact that Incks was involved in a couple of unpleasant scandals with a young boy, then a prostitute – he never seemed to be able to make his mind up which he preferred. The cases were hushed up by the ministry – he was by then too valuable to lose – and he was never taken to court. It's my guess that Margay has blackmailed his weak-willed twin brother into co-operating with him in this new venture.'

As Kate's sons staggered down the stairs rubbing the sleep from their eyes, she rose to serve them breakfast and a stiff warning to be quiet.

'And Vlaxi?' de Troq' asked.

'Probably just there to provide money and muscle. I think Margay realised he was somewhat out of his depth and turned to him for his expert organisation.'

'And the mysterious Cats or Catmen my father referred to?'

'Lynx and Margay,' a small yawning boy said from behind his croissant.

'What do you mean?'

'They're both wild cats,' he replied simply. 'I promise. Look, I'll show you.' He stumbled up the stairs again to return a moment later clutching a large book on wild animals.

'It's in English,' he pointed out as he leafed through the pages, 'but they're in here somewhere.'

The page he finally stopped at showed a collection of drawings of wild cats. 'Serval, lynx, bobcat, jaguar, ocelot, jaguarondi, there it is,' he said excitedly, 'Margay, see!'

No one contradicted the child; it was there in front of them in black and white.

'Which means that my father must have come across one or both of them in Hong Kong.'

'Probably while they were negotiating for the export of the equipment they needed. He's an astute man, your father, Kate,' Pel said. 'He came across something that smelt wrong and kept on digging. Unfortunately they'd covered their tracks well and he wasn't able to find out much more.'

'And the eyes in the stars he referred to in his second message?' de Troq' asked.

'The satellite,' Pel said. 'The piece of paper with all those scribblings on,' he continued, speaking to Pierre. 'We got our experts in Paris to work on it. When they finally deciphered it they suddenly clammed up and nearly arrested our man Debray as a spy.'

'The computer co-ordinates for the weather satellite. The one Incks is going to Toulouse for. The co-ordinates were incomplete but there was enough to identify them.'

'But what does Margay want with those? To sabotage the weather forecasts for the Météo?'

'We don't know yet, but I think not. My guess is it's something more sophisticated than that. In any event, now we can understand why, when Georges stole the documents from Margay's office, his landlady and lover were murdered.'

'And finally Georges too,' Pierre added sadly.

'And finally Georges,' Pel agreed. 'Robbing Margay he stumbled on to something far larger than he had expected. I don't suppose he even realised exactly what.'

It wasn't at all what they had expected. As Pel pointed out, a lot of what he'd told them was supposition; what they really needed was solid evidence. Achieving that was going to be much more difficult.

'Catch them at it,' Pierre suggested.

'Go on.' Pel leaned forward to listen.

'Wait for them to start their little scheme at Incks' house and go in and nab them.'

'But that could be months away.'

'From the look of the set-up in his house, I don't think so. I'm no computer genius, just an electrician, but the whole lot was plugged in and looked ready to go to me. I'll keep watch from the cottage if you like,' he suggested.

'I think, Pierre, you've done enough already.' Pel had a sneaking suspicion that if he found his brother's murderers just across the river from where he was keeping watch, Pierre might dash in. He didn't want another murder on his hands – or the other possibility, Margay getting away after being alerted by Pierre's clumsy attempts at revenge.

'I think I'd better go back and see Commissaire Calvet to inform him of what exactly is going on. We're going to need his help.'

27

Commissaire Calvet listened carefully to Pel's suggested plan and promised his full co-operation. He offered one of his inspectors and a sergeant to keep watch from the cottage. Communication was their main problem: the cottage had no phone and was a long way from anything. Radio telephones were out of the question because Incks would surely pick up whatever was said on his sophisticated apparatus. As they worked their way round the subject Darcy pointed out that leaving two men on the other side of the forest was a tricky business – they might lose themselves trying to get back to let them know what was happening.

'In that case,' Calvet said, 'I'll have to find among my men someone who knows the forest well enough not to get lost.'

It wasn't easy but he finally turned up a young cadet who had been born at Fayzac, not far from Itzac, and who claimed to know the forest like the back of his hand having played there as a boy and, as he told them, blushing, having taken a number of girls there on summer evenings as an adolescent to do romantic things to each other.

'Do you think he's up to it?' Pel asked as Cadet Simon left the office.

'He'd better be,' Calvet replied coldly. Pel nodded in agreement. It was just how he felt.

*

Later that day Kate and Darcy escorted Calvet's inspector and Cadet Simon on borrowed horses through the forest to install them in the cottage. There was no sign of movement across the river and, having shown them where everything was, Darcy and Kate made their way slowly back.

When they arrived at the château, Pel was on the phone.

'News from Debray,' de Troq' told them. 'Something's up.'

They waited patiently to find out exactly what. While they waited Pierre and Jo-jo came in from the yard.

'Am I still under house arrest?' Pierre asked dolefully.

'For the moment,' de Troq' replied. 'Where I go, you go, and vice versa.'

Pel put the phone down. 'They're doing a test run at Toulouse tomorrow evening,' he said. 'Incks has been in Toulouse all day. He'll be there until midday tomorrow. I think we can expect some action tomorrow night. I'll tell Calvet to be ready with his men just in case.'

That night de Troq' accompanied Pierre, his wife and their two small boys back to their house down the lane. After their usual small night-cap they retired to bed. De Troq' slept like a log thanks to the *somnifère* Pierre had slipped into his drink. Pierre kissed his wife and made her promise not to say a word. He climbed through the bedroom window on to the adjoining roof below. He went like a cat across it and landed with a gentle thud on the ground. On his back he had a large rucksack. It was full and heavy, but Pierre was built like an ox and the extra weight was no hindrance as he moved off towards the edge of the forest. The moon was bright and he smiled to himself, knowing that once through the trees and out the other side he wouldn't even need the powerful torch in his pocket.

*

194

The early morning sunlight glinted through the glazed front door to wake de Troq', who had been sleeping so soundly on the large convertible sofa. He got up and began folding the camp bed back into the body of the sofa just as Pierre came down the stairs behind him.

'I thought I heard you moving about,' he said cheerfully. 'I'll make us some coffee.'

Pel and Darcy left for Albi that morning in Kate's large car. Darcy glanced back in the mirror as he manoeuvred the Bentley out of the yard. Damn him, he thought, as he saw de Troq' talking with Kate on the terrace – but at least Pierre and Jo-jo would be there as well, he reassured himself.

During the day they discussed their plans with Commissaire Calvet. He was a sensible man and knew his area well. They pored over the local maps, pin-pointing where they were to station their men.

'Our problem', he said, 'is that there is only one way in and out of Incks' house. They've chosen it well. Getting close is going to be mighty difficult without anyone noticing us. We must assume there'll be someone on watch. I think the last five hundred metres at least must be done on foot. But we'll have a back-up ready in the lane if we need them and more where it joins the road to Montauban, just in case.'

They studied the map together, satisfied that it was all they could do, until Pel noticed the river.

'What about boats?' he said. 'They may just be ready with a couple themselves.'

'I'll get on to it.'

Everything seemed to be ready. Debray confirmed to them from Paris that Incks had done his stuff at Toulouse and had now left the base.

'No point in tailing him,' Calvet said. 'He or one of his colleagues may notice, and anyway, we know where he's going. Their plan can't work unless Incks is there to make it work. It's time we were off. My men have instructions to get themselves into position as soon as it's dark.'

Kate was hopping about in the kitchen eager for her own instructions while Pel, Darcy, de Troq' and Calvet compared notes. Pierre sat glumly on the edge watching them, while Jo-jo busied herself with the over-excited children. They'd never seen so many detectives and were desperate to get in on the act. It was only with outright bribery in the form of a promise of a new video game that they'd been wanting for ages that Kate finally shut them up. At last Jo-jo and Kate took all four of them upstairs to bed.

As she came back down Darcy smiled up at her.

'Can't I do something?' she pleaded in a whisper.

'No one's doing anything at the moment,' he answered, 'but when the time comes you can make sure Pierre stays put.'

'Is that all?'

'It's enough. Pel would never forgive me for allowing you to get mixed up with gun-brandishing bandits.'

She laughed. 'You make it sound like something out of a cowboy film.'

'With Margay the American involved, it easily could be.'

It was just before midnight that Cadet Simon cantered into the yard. Kate had been half-heartedly sulking outside in the warm evening air and was the first to see him.

'He's here,' she shouted to the waiting policemen.

Calvet demanded a report from Simon who, unfortunately, was very out of breath having just galloped the breadth of the forest, only losing his way twice – not that he was going to tell anyone that.

'There's activity,' he gasped at last. 'Two vehicles came

up the track opposite. A number of men got out and went into the house. I can't tell you exactly how many, but we think there were at least six.'

'Looks like the party's started,' Calvet commented. 'I think it's time to go.'

The château emptied. Cadet Simon went off in a car with the others. As Kate led away his sweating horse she quietly wished Darcy good luck, but he didn't reply – he wasn't listening.

As the cars disappeared the yard fell silent.

Kate looked at Pierre and Jo-jo. 'Time to saddle up Bebel and Jess,' she said. 'If we get a move on we'll be there before them.'

'Just hope the bloke at the cottage doesn't cause us any trouble.'

'He won't. He's been instructed to cross the river by rowing-boat and wait on the other side.'

'Good thing I moored mine a bit further along then. They won't have pinched that one.'

Jo-jo waved the two riders off into the darkness and went inside to babysit and bite her nails.

28

The moon was still clear and gave them enough light to see by. Going through the trees had been tricky but with the aid of spots of moonlight which pierced the thick over-head branches and the occasional flash of Pierre's torch they arrived above the cottage in good time and fastened the horses to a couple of trees. As they slid down the bank to the garden to wait, Kate noticed Pierre was clutching a small black plastic box in his hand. It looked suspiciously like the controls to his sons' remote-control car.

From where they sat they could see Incks' house easily. It was even floodlit for the occasion. There was one man with a rifle and a walkie-talkie prowling round outside. Although they knew there was someone sitting in a boat on the other side of the river, as were a number of others further downstream, they couldn't see anyone else. Everyone was well hidden. Now they just had to wait.

They didn't see Pel and his party arrive at first.

They heard a shot being fired from the prowling guard then there was a stampede of feet on the hard-baked ground and a dozen silhouettes ran forward from the track towards the house. As the guard fired again he was shouting into his dangling walkie-talkie, 'Cut the juice!'

A moment later the river bank was in darkness. After the intense light of the exterior lamps no one could see a thing. The police stopped dead, completely blinded by the blackness that enfolded them like a hideous smothering blanket.

'I knew the bastards would do that,' Pierre said to nobody in particular and lifted the little black box up in front of his face, squinting to see what he was doing. He flicked a switch and a small pin-point of light came on. It was working.

'Here goes.' He manipulated a small dial from left to right and held his breath. 'It's got to work, please God let it work.'

There was a lot of shouting in the darkness but nothing else.

Pierre wrenched the dial to left and right, cursing under his breath.

Suddenly there was a terrific flash, followed by a number of loud explosions. For a moment everyone thought they were being shot at and threw themselves to the ground. The explosions continued, to be joined by a wonderful display of cascading fireworks. They lit the whole river bank with fountains of red, blue, green and yellow lights.

'Pierre!' Darcy said to himself as he shouted to the men clutching the ground behind him. 'Get yourselves into the house,' he screamed, leaping to his feet and running full tilt for the still-open door. The inhabitants were nonplussed. Some of them were trying to get out of the house to see what was happening, some were trying to get in under cover, the whole lot of them were firing willy-nilly into the night at their non-existent assailants. Still the fireworks continued. The boatmen moved quickly upriver and scaled the steep banks to reinforce the team already there. By the time they'd managed to scramble their way up it was almost over. Someone switched the floodlights back on and gradually the firework display subsided. Pierre dropped his gadget and made for his boat. He was determined to thump someone for depriving him of his brother. Two cars filled with policemen screeched to a halt in the quietening chaos.

The police had taken control and were lining up their arrests against the wall of the house. It was then that Kate saw him.

A single shadow creeping through the undergrowth.

It slid down the riverside and climbed into Pierre's boat. Gradually the rowing boat made its way silently across towards her.

She crouched in the bushes, hoping not to be seen.

In the calm after the storm Pel was counting heads.

'There's someone missing,' he said to Calvet.

A shot rang out in the sudden silence. A horse whinnied.

'Kate!' Pierre had stopped twisting the arm he was holding and had spun round to stare across the river at the cottage.

But it was Darcy who ran full tilt to skid down the bank and land with his feet in the river.

He recovered himself and scrambled into the policemen's abandoned boat. He cast off and rowed furiously for the opposite side.

Leaving the boat floating free he leapt for the overhanging scrub, flinging himself at the river bank and clutching at prickly branches that stabbed at his hands. He found a foothold and started climbing.

It didn't look far but it took an eternity, as if there was a great weight dragging him back towards the river.

At last he was upright and pushing his way blindly through the undergrowth towards the cottage.

Pel ordered one of the floodlights to be hauled round in the direction of the gunshot. As the lamp swung round, Darcy saw a body in the long grass.

'Kate!'

'I'm here,' she said, calmly stepping out of the shadows.

Darcy stopped dead in his tracks, seeing Kate safe and smiling.

'Then who in hell's name is that?'

'Incks, I suppose.'

'It can't be Incks, he burst into tears when Pel arrested him. This must be Margay.'

He turned the body over with his foot. It was Margay, although his face had been heavily dented. In any event, he was very unconscious.

'What happened?' Darcy said, staring at the broken cowboy.

'I hit him.'

'What with, for God's sake, a piece of lead piping you happened to be carrying about your person?'

'No, my fist.'

'Your fist? Christ!'

'Certainly, a woman in *la France profonde* has to learn to defend herself, *n'est ce pas?*' She laughed. 'I guess I overdid it a bit, didn't I?'

'I think you've broken his jaw, not to mention the rest.' Darcy grinned at her. 'Thank God I never tried to make a pass at you. I might have lost the rest of my teeth.'

'You thought about making a pass at me?'

'Fairly regularly.'

'If I promise not to cosh you, would you think about it again?'

As Darcy took Kate in his arms and kissed her passionately, they were caught, like two actors in the final embrace just before the curtain drops, in the beam of light from the other side of the river. Pel sighed and turned away. Darcy was back to normal. The other policemen couldn't resist it. Led by de Troq', they vigorously applauded the embrace to the accompaniment of cat-calls.

*

'It was only a test run after all,' Pel said, sitting comfortably on the terrace of Château Coste. That day, all day, they had wrapped the case up. As he stretched wearily in the sinking sun, letting the warmth seep into his aching bones, he addressed his team.

'This morning everyone had verbal diarrhoea – we've got the whole story now. Georges robbed Margay of the precious papers and immediately tried to sell them back. Margay's heavy mob, in searching for Georges, left their trail of destruction: Madame Marty, Lulu Lafon, Monsieur Marty and finally poor Georges. With the co-ordinates Incks supplied and the electronic equipment they'd imported and set up, under cover of Margay's request to open a factory up north, they were going to plug into the computers at Toulouse and do their own bit of surveillance. Not just the weather, either – with Incks' expertise they intended to connect themselves up to various other computers and sell information about locations to commercial competitors in the EC. And I've been informed', he added, 'that it would have been possible, if they had someone clever enough to do it, and they did, to get into the European stock exchanges. It would have been better than robbing a dozen banks. No wonder Vlaxi was showing an interest in the Bourse.'

'And Margay?'

'He's finding it difficult to say anything at the moment, with his jaw in plaster.' He smiled broadly at Kate, managing to look less dyspeptic than usual. 'But he did give us the name of our stiletto murderer. Sittingwell, his American associate, will be doing a long spell in a very uncomfortable French prison. Patterson and Goldberg'll be going away too, and poor old Incks hasn't stopped sobbing yet. He was the brains but without the ideas. When he discovered he had a real brother he fell on him full of joy and did exactly as he was told. He's another one we won't be seeing for quite some time – he's going to go on being the missing L. Incks for a good deal longer. The

202

only one that got away was Vlaxi – as slippery as an eel, that one, and ten times as nasty. He hasn't been seen since the fourteenth of July. He'll turn up, though whether we'll be able to pin anything on him is a different matter. Even Margay is keeping his mouth shut about him.'

That evening, at Château Coste, was riotous. Inevitably, Pierre and Jo-jo arrived with their two boys to add some weight to the already growing noise. Pierre knew he would have to go to court for the robbery of Margay Manor, but under the circumstances, it was felt he would get off lightly, particularly with Pel to speak up about his help with the final arrests. If it hadn't been for his timely interference they might have lost the lot.

It had been a copious meal at the long table on the terrace. Kate had gone to the trouble of choosing the wine carefully – all from Burgundy, naturally, to save arguments from Pel that the Tarn producers weren't up to scratch, although she'd noticed he'd polished off a fair number of glassfuls during his stay. The gathering was animated. Everyone was there, even Commissaire Calvet, and they were still excitedly discussing their success, particularly the children, who had had nothing to do with it at all. The only person who was silent, unusually, was Pel, who sat leaning against the back of his chair at the head of the table, his spectacles poised on his forehead and a sickly smile on his face. As Darcy glanced at him he had the suspicion that his boss might just be feeling pleased too.

'Happy, patron?' he said.

Pel leaned forward abruptly to snatch up a cigarette from the table, his spectacles snapping back into place on his nose as if he were closing the windows.

'Happy?' he replied, as he lit his cigarette viciously. 'Have you thought of the backlog of work that's been piling up back at the Hôtel de Police while we've been down here?' He sniffed. Pel could say a lot with a sniff. 'It'll be Christmas before we've caught up again.'

'Perhaps we should set off this evening,' Darcy suggested. 'You could be in the office first thing in the morning that way.'

Pel scowled at him, then at everyone else. 'With my stomach, that would be suicide after such a rich meal. No,' he said, helping himself to another piece of Camembert, which was trying to slide off the plate on its own, 'we're just going to have to wait until tomorrow morning.'